I0712939

DEAD SCIENCE

Edited by

A.P. FUCHS

COSCOM ENTERTAINMENT
WINNIPEG

COSCOM ENTERTAINMENT
130 Stanier Street
Winnipeg, MB R2L 1N3 Canada

This book is a work of fiction. Names, characters, places and events either are products of the authors' imagination or are used fictitiously. Any resemblance to actual places, events or persons living or dead or living dead is purely coincidental.

ISBN – 10 1-897217-85-4
ISBN – 13 978-1-897217-85-6

All stories contained herein are Copyright © 2009 by their respective authors. All rights reserved, including the right to reproduce in whole or in part in any form or medium.

PUBLISHED BY COSCOM ENTERTAINMENT
www.coscomentertainment.com
Text set in Garamond; Printed and bound in the USA
COVER ART BY SCOTT STORY
EDITED BY A.P. FUCHS

Library and Archives Canada Cataloguing in Publication

Dead science : a zombie anthology / edited by A.P. Fuchs ; Glen Held ... [et al.].

ISBN 978-1-897217-85-6

1. Horror tales, American.   2. American fiction--21st century. 3. Horror tales. I. Fuchs, A. P. (Adam Peter), 1980- II. Held, Glen

PN6071.H727D39 2009   813'.087380806   C2009-902159-5

DEAD SCIENCE

SASHIMI Á LA MORTE
by
LORNE DIXON

Doctor Silas Drundtl stood under the flickering parking garage lights, fanned out his keys in his palm, and wondered which would open his car door. The batteries inside his keychain remote were dead. For the first time since buying the luxury sedan, he would have to use its key.

Unfortunately, he didn't have the slightest clue what most of the keys in his hand opened. He recognized the keys to his house, his office, and his safety security and post office boxes, but that left a half dozen more. He hated his need to hang on to things.

Silas closed his fist around the keychain, dropped his head and closed his eyes. It had been too long a day, three procedures, with one that ended with him telling a sixty-five-year-old woman that she was a widow. He needed to drink a cheap domestic beer in his bed and let the sound of the air conditioner lull him to sleep.

"Drundtl? Is your name Silas Drundtl?"

Opening his eyes, he turned towards the voice. It belonged to a tall wire sculpture in a designer suit and bifocals. Behind him, two greasy bodybuilders in European dress shirts stood with arms crossed. The trio didn't have the word "criminals" tattooed on their foreheads—that would have been too subtle—but Silas assumed the word was inked on their hearts.

When he didn't immediately answer, the man asked, "Don't you speak English? I can probably accommodate. I speak six languages. I do international law."

One of the thugs asked, "You Drundtl or what?"

"Why do you ask?" he said, and realized at the same moment that "Never heard of him" was probably a better response.

The tall man's head bobbed like a peacock when he spoke. "*I'm* not asking. Enzo Occhialini, my boss, he's the one who's asking. You just imagine him standing right here between Guili and Cesare."

Silas inched towards the men. He knew Occhialini's name from the weekly   papers—retired-billionaire-cold-war-biochemist-turned-seafood-restaurateur—with multiple indictments for money laundering and extortion. "And your name?"

The peakcock's head shot straight up. "I'm Mr. Fitcher."

Fitcher extended his hand. Their eyes locked and Silas stared into two swirling black holes. In most men's eyes there were hints of their humanity—a twinkling of humor, a gleam of nobility and purpose. Fitcher had the eyes of a corpse. Silas took the offered hand and shook it.

"Tonight you'll make one hundred thousand dollars for a couple hours work," Fitcher said, pupils dilating like a high tech guidance system locking in on a target. "Our car is waiting."

There was no threat issued, not verbally or with body language, but there was no mistake, either—this was not a job offer to be accepted or refused. With Guili and Cesare flanking him, Silas followed Fitcher to an idling limousine.

They didn't speak as the driver sped them through the city, hurrying through yellow lights, ignoring crosswalks. After a few minutes, Silas turned away from the window and stared at his feet. He imagined them encased in cement, dangling off a lower east side pier.

The car pulled into a private driveway through a pair of arched wrought iron gates into Occhialini's estate. As it glided to a gentle halt, Silas asked Fitcher, "Why does he want *me*? I win the lottery or something?"

A wry grin wormed its way over Fitcher's face. "Mr. Occhialini's personal physician died recently after a long illness."

"What did he have?"

Opening the door, Fitcher said, "It's a very common disease called infidelity. I believe he caught it from Mrs. Occhialini. In the end, it proved fatal."

Silas stepped out of the limousine and followed Fitcher past a long rose garden, up marble stairs and through the mansion's mahogany doors. Guili shut and locked the entrance behind them. In the massive main hall, Cesare took Silas's coat and handed it to a servant dressed entirely in white. They corralled him through a maze of rooms—parlors, barrooms and lounges—to a large dinning hall.

Occhialini, stick figure thin, sat at the head of a long Ash Birch banquet table. There were no other place settings or chairs. Fitcher nodded to his boss and announced, "This is Dr. Drundtl."

"I read your paper in *The New England Journal of Medicine*," Occhialini said as he unfolded a cloth napkin, freeing a pair of silver chopsticks. "The one about metabolic relativism."

Silas squinted, his mind blank, and then shrugged. "Oh. That actually wasn't my work. There's another Silas Drundtl down in Princeton—"

Occhialini dropped the chopsticks. "You didn't write the article? You're not the guy?"

"No."

Fitcher's eyes flicked between Occhialini and Silas.

"Did you even read that article?"

Silas took his time before nodding. "Yes."

"Did you agree with the findings?"

Silas saw Fitcher nod, an almost unperceivable instruction to agree, but said, "Not really. But I'm a surgeon, not a—"

"Well, that's a relief, actually," Occhialini said, replacing the fork. "'Cause I think that fool is dead wrong. I chose him for tonight to teach him a thing or two. But, you know, since you're already here."

Silas blinked. "Here for what?"

"Dinner." Occhialini clapped.

A team of Japanese chefs rolled a large aquarium into the dinning hall. The fish inside, half buried in sand, was almost a foot and a half long and covered with flesh-colored plates. Almost flat, it resembled an eyeless catfish suited up in armor, except for the teeth on display when its wide mouth opened. No catfish had incisors like that.

"What *is* that?" Silas asked.

Fitcher tapped the glass and the fish darted to the aquarium wall, teeth gnashing, scales rising. "It was called Phyllolepis. A fresh water fish extinct since the Devonian age. Well, extinct until now. An intact specimen was discovered on the banks of the Guyandotte River, perfectly preserved in an alluvial fan ridge. It's an incredibly rare find, a naturally mummified creature with DNA strands intact. Enough to clone this fellow."

The fish circled in the tank, now agitated.

"I'm a seafood connoisseur. I've had delicacies that only kings and pontiffs have tasted. The finest caviar from early season Caspian Sea Sturgeon. The belly of the endangered unarmored three-spine Stickleback. Even giant squid, though that in itself is another story. But the Phyllolepis is different. No man has ever tasted its flesh."

The fish settled back into the sand.

"Or would survive," Fitcher said. "We took diagnostic samples from our friend here. Its flesh contains a cocktail of powerful neurotoxins."

"And you intend to eat it anyway?" Silas asked.

Occhialini smiled. "I do."

"And you're here to keep him alive." Fitcher stepped away from the tank and nodded to the lead chef. He rolled a pair of mesh gloves up his arms.

"Wait. No," Silas said, raising both hands. "I don't know the first thing about the toxins. I don't have the pharmaceuticals or know dosages. I haven't even examined—"

Fitcher hushed him and pointed. Against the far wall was a mini-bar stocked with medical supplies. "You'll find everything you need right there. All of the medicine vials have been prepared for Mr. Occhialini's age and weight."

Silas's eyes scanned the mini-bar. It was an impressive—and blatantly illegal—collection. "I still can't."

Occhialini rolled his eyes. "Are you going to make us go out and find some other doctor? 'Cause I'm hungry and getting impatient. If 'no' is your final answer, that's fine."

He pointed a chopstick at Guili. "Take him out back. I don't want a mess like that time with that incompetent repairman. I had to fly those linen cleaners in from Naples."

Guili took Silas by the shirt collar, twisted, and lifted him off the floor. His arms flexed, revealing a roadmap of purple veins and arteries. He snarled. "Boss's pocket watch was still off by four seconds after he *fixed* it, so I got to *fix* him. Did too good a job."

Occhialini slid the watch out of his coat pocket. "It's an 1898 A. Lange And Söhne not some mass produced Rolex trash, a watch worth treasuring, worth killing for."

"Agreed," Fitcher said.

Both hands around Guili's wrists, Silas croaked, "Wait. I'll do it. I'll do it. I'lldoit."

Occhialini gestured for Guili to release him and snickered as the doctor dropped, fell to his knees, and rubbed his neck. "Thank you, Doctor."

Fitcher turned to the chefs and said, "Let's start."

The lead chef reached into the tank. The Phyllolepis darted out of the sand, needle-filled mouth open, and attached itself to the chef's glove. The chef yelled and withdrew his hand, pulling the fish out of the tank. Slamming it down on the table, he tried to catch its tail with his free hand. He screamed as its scales sliced into his fingers.

The second chef took his position at the table, angling a raised meat clever over the fish's body as it flopped back and forth, tearing through the glove. He swung down, striking the Phyllolepis just below its smooth, bulbous head. Pressing down, he decapitated it.

The lead chef pried the dead fish's mouth open and slid out of the mesh glove. A few of the needle-like teeth remained imbedded in his ruined hand. He swore in Japanese, bowed towards Occhialini, and ran from the room.

"Spirited fish," Occhialini said.

Fitcher cracked his knuckles. "Had some fight in it."

The second chef waited for the fish to move before carving it with a long takohiki knife. He cleaned the fish quickly, scaling off the armor plates, shaving off skin and fat, and slicing off a series of one-inch-thick fillets. He spread out three slices on a square plate garnished with lime slices, bamboo shoots and seaweed. The chef slid the plate in front of Occhialini, bowed, and stepped away.

Occhialini took a sip of lemon water to clear his palate. He fumbled with his chopsticks, grinned and said, "Excuse me, I'm just excited."

Capturing a fillet between the shaking sticks, he brought it to his lips. The flesh wiggled as he sucked it into his mouth. He chewed.

"How's it taste, Boss?" Cesare asked.

Occhialini swallowed, took another sip of water, then turned to Cesare and said, "Difficult to describe. Nothing like modern fish. Meatier . . . more . . ."

Occhialini fell silent. There were two indications that he wasn't just searching for words to describe the cuisine. His white-knuckled fists slapping to his chest was the first. His eyes were the second hint. They exploded.

Guili blurted out a short, ugly word and took an unconscious step away from the table.

Convulsing, Occhialini collapsed onto the table and slid until the chair under him tipped over. He hit the floor, arms curled up over his chest like a dead bird. He stopped twitching.

Fitcher ran to Silas, put a hand on his back and pushed him towards his boss. Prodding him farther, Fitcher screamed, "Help him. HELP HIM NOW—"

Silas broke out of his shock and rushed to the fallen man, not out of the threat of violence or the promised payment for his services, but because he was a doctor. Kneeling, he put a hand on Occhialini's throat and felt the man's pulse wither down to a weak occasional pump. "I need a defibrillator and an Epinephrine syringe."

The goons exchanged empty stares.

Silas pointed. "The crash cart."

Fitcher reached it first and rolled it over.

Silas pumped Occhialini's chest with his palms.

"What do I do?" Fitcher asked.

Silas took one hand off Occhialini's chest and gestured to the defibrillator's power cord. "Plug it in."

Eager to help, Cesare snatched up the plug and ran towards the bar. The cord, still wound around the defibrillator's base, snapped tripwire tight. The cart overturned, spilling the defibrillator, boxes of medical gloves and dozens of syringes across the floor.

Fitcher screamed, "IDIOT."

Silas continued CPR even though he could no longer feel a pulse.

Cesare scrambled, still searching for a wall socket, dragging the defibrillator behind him. Guili chased the machine, hunched over, hands scraping the floor, trying to free the cord. He slid on a latex glove and fell screaming onto a bed of hypodermic needles.

"Idiots," Fitcher muttered.

Silas pulled his hands off Occhialini, stood, and turned to Fitcher. "It's not going to matter. He's dead."

Cesare and Guili ran to Fitcher's side.

"You can resus—"

"—bring him back with the paddles—"

"—ain't, you know, *dead* dead, right?"

Silas firmly shook his head. "He's *dead* dead, yes."

Cesare's eyes filled with tears. He dropped the defibrillator. It crashed to the floor, crushing syringes, its hard plastic case cracking. "You gotta do something. You gotta, man."

Silas said, "There's nothing I can—"

Cesare's hands came down on Silas's shoulders like bolts of lightning. He lifted the doctor off the floor and tossed him onto the dining table, pushing into his throat with a bulbous elbow. He shook Silas and spat as he spoke. "The boss took me in when I was seven *after my father died*. He treated me like . . . *like a son* . . . taught me everything he could. I was never real smart. I was never gonna be a boss like him, but that never . . . that *never* mattered to him. He treated me like a son—"

Silas sputtered, unable to respond, and flailed his arms. Intense heat swam up from his throat. His lungs began to twitch as they tried to expel the depleted oxygen trapped within. Cesare's face began to darken as consciousness began to fail.

Cesare turned, his mouth dropped open, and he lifted himself off Silas. Silas pushed himself across the table, out from under the thug's shadow, hacked out a series of rapid coughs. He turned his head.

Occhialini sat up.

Cesar bolted to his side, slid onto his knees and wrapped his large arms around his boss. "You okay now, Boss? You scared the hell out of us. He said you was dead, y'know, *dead* dead."

Occhialini's head snapped to one side, pivoted to face Cesare, and smiled. Dozens of sharp teeth no wider than needles had sprouted in his mouth. He launched his jaws into Cesare's face, biting down, lacerating open a gaping hole. Cesare's face disappeared in one bite, replaced by a hollow red cavity that exposed the skull underneath.

The skull face screamed as Occialini's head whipped back, tearing the wound open even further. The boss's tongue snaked out, twined itself around the flap of flesh dangling from his mouth, and sucked it in.

Fitcher backed away until he was against the kitchen door. Guili pulled a handgun out of a leather holster under his jacket, aimed it at his boss, and said, "Get away from him, Mr. O. I don't wanna have shoot at you, but you gotta get away from him. He needs a doctor. He—"

Guili spun on his heels, eyebrows raised, and pointed at Silas. Still sprawled across the table, Silas flinched. Guili yelled, *"You're* a doctor. You get over there and help him. He needs—"

Silas shook his head.

Occhialini tossed Cesare's body to the floor and stood up. Guili turned, waving the gun between Silas and his boss. *"You,* Boss, you don't move. *You,* Doc, move."

Silas reached out for one of the chopsticks.

Occhialini rushed towards Guili.

Guili screamed and fired. Two slugs pounded through Occhialini's chest. The shots drilled right through, sending twin jet streams of blood twirling behind him, but the boss didn't lose any momentum. He leaped onto Guili, arms grappling, head cocked back, toothy mouth open. Guili landed a single punch across Occhialini's chin a second before the dead man's face burrowed into his neck. Guili dropped to the floor in a shower of fluid.

Silas wrapped his hands around the chopstick, dropped off the table and drove it into Occhialini's gut. The dead man's arm snapped up, slapping him away with incredible force. Silas fled.

Occhialini tore the chopstick out of his body. A five–inch–long intestinal tapeworm wriggled on its end, impaled but still alive.

Membrane separated as the tapeworm grew a snarling mouth on both ends, filled with tiny teeth.

The boss dropped the chopstick. The worm freed itself and slithered across the floor, heading for Silas.

Cesare's body rose from the floor, eye liquefying and running down the creases of his face. Guili stopped shuddering and stood up. He tore his eyeballs out of their sockets and chewed on them with his new teeth.

Fitcher swore in every one of the six languages he spoke. Silas only spoke English, but he understood each word perfectly.

Silas sprinted for the door. Fitcher followed close behind, arms swinging as he ran. Silas glanced back and saw the dead men shambling across the floor like a trio of angry drunks. Guili's size-eleven shoe came down on the tapeworm. It shrieked and squirmed; its body flattened under his heel.

They sped through the cocktail lounge, their feet landing hard on the polished cherry hardwood, and into another spacious room furnished with plush leather sofas and a massive television. Fitcher slipped on a loose roll of medical gauze partially unfurled on the floor. Catching his balance, he avoided tumbling over an overturned first aid kit.

There were pools of blood on the largest sofa. Silas reacted first, skidding away from the bloodshed, his eyes focusing on the two bodies tangled on the floor just ahead of the furniture. The lead chef burrowed into his subordinate's chest with both hands, digging like a dog tunneling under a fence, tearing open a wide crater. His lips were smeared with blood, an ugly red line, like a prostitute's lipstick after a quick twenty-dollar transaction.

Occhialini and his men broke into the room, desperate hands slapping against the door frame, noses twitching as they sniffed the air. Their foreheads had melted down over their eyes, leaving a crest of thick wrinkles just above their cheekbones. Silas thought of the Phyllolepis's smooth, eyeless head, but only for a moment. He cut across the room, Fitcher trailing, then through a white door.

"Not *left*," Fitcher screamed, but it was too late. Silas had already spun through a second door. The lawyer stopped, hands spread. "Not in there."

Guili's hands grabbed Fitcher from behind, jerking him back. Silas reached out and caught hold of his hands, planted his feet against the door's molding, and pulled. Fitcher screamed. Cesare rounded the corner and dove headfirst on top of Fitcher, burying his teeth in the older man's shoulder, tearing through his shirt and the loose flesh underneath.

Fitcher's scream ended as the strain on his vocal cords grew too intense and his voice failed.

Grunting, Silas leaned hard against the wall and pulled on Fitcher's arms.

Cesare bit down deeper. Silas heard bone snap.

Occhialini appeared over his henchmen's shoulders, grinning through a thick forest of needle-thin teeth.

Silas yelled and jerked hard on Fitcher's hands.

Fitcher came loose from their grasp and they fell into the room. Silas barely noticed that Fitcher's arm remained in the hallway, dangling from Cesare's mouth. It seemed to wave to them as Silas slammed the door shut, locking the monsters out.

Fitcher's hand covered the stump at his shoulder. He made hoarse little yelping sounds with every hyperventilating exhale.

The monsters pounded on the door. The dead goons were big men. Silas knew it wouldn't take much time for them to get through. He stood up, intending to survey the room for weapons. He didn't get the chance. Shock struck him, freezing him in place, until the sound of the wooden door cracking returned him to his senses. He asked Fitcher, "What is this?"

"It was . . . was an indoor . . . spa . . . but . . ."

Only a few feet into the room the tile floor descended into a massive pool. A massive filtration system hummed. On the bottom of the pool Silas saw dozens of Phyllolepis swimming in lazy circles.

". . . can't clone . . . just one . . . gotta clone . . . a whole . . ."

On the other side of the spa pool there was a set of glass doors leading out to a deck. Silas's eyes darted to the walls. There were only narrow ledges, maybe three inches thick, on either side of the water.

". . . school."

The door began to splinter. The dead were breaking through.

Silas bent down and tried to pry Fitcher off the floor. "Come on, you have to help me. We've got to get across—"

Fitcher shook his head. His face paled. "We both know . . . I'm not . . . going any . . . where."

The door gave way in a shower of wood splinters. Occhialini stepped over the threshold, a long tongue slithering out from between quivering lips.

Silas released Fitcher and scurried to the east wall. He stepped onto the ledge, hand flat against the tile wall, and carefully took three quick steps. He felt his weight shift and his knees wobble, but he kept his balance.

Occhialini pounced on Fitcher, hands and teeth tearing. Fitcher grappled with his employer, not pushing him away but pulling him close. They began to roll. The two men splashed into the shallow end of the pool, blood seeping into the water. Guili and Cesare followed, wading in, chasing down the slope to the deep end, until the water reached their waists.

The Phyllolepis swarmed towards the men.

Silas took another step. He saw Fitcher nod under water, signaling him, a moment before a fish latched over one eye and Occhialini tore out his throat.

Trembling, Silas put his left foot in front of his right. The battle in the shallower water had created a tide. Waves crashed over the ledge. Silas's right foot slipped as he took another step.

He plunged into the water.

Underwater, he saw half of the Phyllolepis turn and swim towards him, a volley of arrows shot from a line of artillery bows. He kicked off the bottom and swam, arms stretched out in wide arcs, towards the end of the pool.

He felt the first bite just as he broke the water's surface. The teeth felt like a dozen ribbed barbs, cutting deep into his right knee at crossed angles. He bit down on his bottom lip and flailed out his arms, swimming towards the edge. Another bite, this one lower on his leg but deeper, severing muscle. The next four fish hit his body higher, tearing into his abdomen. He tasted arterial blood in the water, his own, and something worse. He realized one of the Phyllolepis had bitten through a loop of intestine, spilling acid and waste into the pool.

Silas reached up and felt the tile ledge at the end of the pool. He pulled himself up, the fish still attached, and fell to the dry tiles. He felt himself fading as he crawled through the glass doors. The fish ate, devouring him, working themselves inside his body, traveling up his digestive tract.

On the other side of the pool, Occhialini wrestled Fitcher's remains from the water and dragged the corpse out the doorway.

Silas's eyes grew hot. He knew he was dying—and changing. Out over the balcony he saw the long driveway leading down to the street.

The lead chef, his coat stained with blood, stumbled past the estate's gates and headed out into the city.

Silas closed his eyes and felt them liquefy.

Sashimi Á la Morte

The last human thoughts that flickered through his head before death and prehistoric instinct took over were directed to Occhialini. *I lied. I did write that paper on metabolic relativism. Maybe you didn't understand it. So here it is, served up cold: You really are what you eat. And you know what? If I can control my actions even a little bit after I die, I promise you this: I will hunt you down, I will eat you, and I will be you.*

ARCH ENEMY
by
GLEN HELD

"Tell me again about the dream, Stan," Joey said, his enormous frame taking up the entire office doorway.

I sighed; Joey always wanted to hear our plans for the future when he didn't want to concentrate on other things. That was okay *this time* since we hadn't had a customer for the last two hours and he'd just about cleaned everything up. Not that there was much to clean. Ever since the new highway opened, traffic in our little out of the way franchise was a quarter of what it had been and, at this time of night, virtually non-existent.

"It's like this," I began, "as soon as we save enough money and I graduate college, we're going to open our own restaurant. It won't be a crummy little franchise like this dump. It'll be a real restaurant, a nice place where people can sit down and enjoy a good meal. It's going to be big, biggest restaurant you've ever laid eyes on and the most beautiful, too."

"And we're going to be the bosses, right?" he asked.

"Right," I said, and he smiled.

"Thanks, Stan, that's all I wanted to hear," Joey said. "You're a good friend."

And, still smiling, he was gone.

At twenty-seven past midnight, Joey returned to my office. I knew that was the time since I had been staring at the cell phone display and counting down the minutes until I could shut down this miserable place for the night. The cell was Joey's which I had borrowed because I'd forgotten mine.

I sighed. "What now?"

"There's a guy knocking at the front door," he said.

"Tell him to go to the drive-thru."

Joey shrugged and left. Although franchise rules called for a minimum of four on duty at night, there was only the two of us. Haradakis, the owner, paid Joey and me extra for that, but only enough to keep us from complaining.

Twelve thirty-two. I put down my car keys that I'd been playing with and decided to check my emails on Haradakis's computer. Two minutes later, I looked up from the machine. Joey had returned.

"I told him like you said, but he won't go away," Joey told me, "and I think there's something wrong with him. He looks sick."

Joey moved aside as I got up. It's been that way since we met in elementary school. In our relationship, I'm the boss; the brains to his brawn. I watch out for him and he has my back.

With Joey lumbering behind me, I walked toward the front of our small restaurant where a figure was knocking at the door. "Inside's closed," I yelled. "Only drive-up's open." But the guy didn't listen. Instead, he started to yank harder at the locked doors. I got a good look at him. "Ugh!" He wore clothes way too big for him and he looked like he'd spent the better part of the summer in a dumpster.

"Should I call the cops?" Joey asked and fumbled around in his pocket. "Where is . . . . Oh yeah, you have my cell."

"Joey, we call the cops and we'll never be left here alone again," I said, although if traffic didn't pick up, the restaurant would soon be closed anyway. "We—" I looked back at the bum and saw the door starting to come off its hinges under the constant pulling. If that door broke, Haradakis would take it out of my paycheck or maybe just fire me outright. And I wouldn't put it past him to blackball me from working anywhere around here again. No way was I going to let that happen. I moved forward and opened the door.

"I told you to get out of here!" Before I could say another word, the freak rushed me. I tried to get out of his way, but the attack was too sudden. I went down, the guy falling on top of me. Drool rolled out of his mouth and onto my chest. My lungs almost exploded from his stink. Choking, I put up my arm to ward him off. I snatched it back quickly as I saw his mouth open and lips pull back.

He was trying to bite me!

The guy lunged forward, but his progress stopped almost as soon as it had begun. "Leave him alone!" Joey roared and ripped him off me. Then my friend carried the squirming intruder to the open door and flung him onto the sidewalk. "Don't come back or you'll get worse!"

Joey's voice was menacing, but that didn't amount to much since the guy lay unmoving where he had landed.

Joey and I looked at each other then slowly walked over to the fallen man. I nudged him with my toe, but he didn't stir.

"I didn't mean to hurt him," Joey whispered. "I was just scared what he might do to you."

I bent down and took hold of the guy's wrist. Nothing. Cautiously, I put my hand to the bum's neck. My blood went ice cold. "I don't think his heart's beating."

"He's dead?" Joey looked at me with fear in his eyes. "I didn't mean to kill him, Stan. I would never kill anybody."

"I know," I said and got to my feet. Now what were we going to do?

"Hey, I know this guy!" Joey suddenly said. "He's the e-nerd."

"E-nerd?"

"Elephant nerd." He shook his head up and down. "When I worked days, there was this big, fat guy who ate three Appeal Meals for lunch every day. He'd eat one and then buy two more fifteen minutes later. He was always alone and always typing away on some sort of computer. That's how he got the name."

I looked at the still-unmoving body and saw the way the skin hung off its face. I guess that also explained the loose clothing.

"I remember hearing somebody on days say they hadn't seen him for a while," Joey continued. "Something bad must have happened to him."

"No, something bad has happened to us." How much trouble would we be in for killing someone whether it was intentional or not? We could kiss off the idea of either of us owning a restaurant after this.

Suddenly, Joey's huge body tensed and his face grew dark. "You're not going to call the cops on me, are you, Stan?" he asked. Although we had been friends for years, I didn't know how he would react if I said yes.

"Of course not."

Joey relaxed then gave me a puzzled look as I again crouched down next to the body. "What are you doing, Stan?" he asked, as I rifled through the guy's pockets.

"Looking for some sort of identification." From inside his coat, I pulled out a rectangular object. But the thing wasn't a wallet. It was a thin, golden case embossed with the word NEXT. Inside were two glass syringes, a dark liquid in each, and an indentation for a missing third needle. Suddenly, the liquid began to glow emerald green.

"I found his wallet in his pants," Joey said, holding out the e-nerd's wallet. Then he saw what I had. "What's that?"

I closed the case and put it in my own pocket. If this guy was on drugs, that would be a big help in our defense.

"Nothing," I said, not wanting to give Joey false hope.

I took the dirty wallet and searched through it. Inside were a few bills and an identification card from someplace called Next Defense Systems with a picture of one fat slob named Robert Binder: The e-nerd.

Whatever.

I shoved the wallet into the e-nerd's coat.

"Let's take him inside before someone sees us," I said.

Although most of the businesses in the area had closed down or weren't open this time of night, I wasn't taking any chances.

I grabbed Binder's corpse under the arms and Joey took his feet. We hoisted him up and headed inside. But no more than two steps inside, Joey dropped his end and stared at the body.

"Are you crazy?" I asked, then let go of my side as well.

The e-nerd's eyes were open.

"Meal," Binder said in a thick voice as he shakily got to his feet.

Relief washed through me. "He's not dead; he's just hungry," I said, although I could have sworn he was lifeless a few moments earlier. "Heat up an Appeal Meal, Stan. We'll give Binder something to eat then boot him out of here."

Joey's face was all smiles as he ran to the kitchen to do what I said. Maybe our dreams were okay after all.

"Listen," I said to the e-nerd, "I don't need any trouble so I'll give you a meal on the house and then you're out of here, okay?"

Unsteady on his feet, the e-nerd just kind of looked at me. I couldn't tell from his eyes whether or not he understood what I had said, but it looked as though something had seeped in. If it hadn't, then Joey would have to throw him out again, this time a lot further.

"Here's the Appeal Meal," Joey said, holding a bag out in front of him. "I made it to-go."

And that's when things started to go crazy. "Must think!" the e-nerd suddenly screamed out, then began to punch himself in the head. Little bits of dirt and filth flew off as he did. Joey backed away, but I just stood there as the e-nerd, eyes once again turning glassy, ran at me with teeth bared.

Once more I found myself on the ground and once more Joey came to my aid, grabbing the e-nerd by the back of his filthy coat and pulling him away from me. Binder fought like a wildcat, but Joey had the size and leverage. He put the e-nerd into a headlock, then threw him into the office and slammed the door shut.

Joey staggered back and I quickly leapt forward to grab the door handle. I held it tight as the e-nerd screamed and tugged at the other side of the portal. I didn't let go, even after the noises inside the office stopped. Then . . .

Click.

I let go of the door as what had happened dawned on me. Quickly, I stopped pulling at the door and tried to open it, but it wouldn't budge. The e-nerd had locked it and if he ruined things in there, we would be finished for sure.

I turned to yell for Joey to help me bust it down, only to find my friend now sitting at a table with his head bowed. I sped over to find tears streaming down his face.

"What's the matter?"

Joey didn't answer. Instead, he continued to soundlessly cry and look down. I followed his gaze to see his arms covered with bleeding, jagged wounds.

It appeared the e-nerd had bitten him.

"It burns," Joey said, turning his sad gaze to me. "It burns real bad."

My heartbeat increased as Joey's face grew white and his breathing slowed. "I'll get you to a doctor," I said, then cursed. My keys were in the office along with the cell phone and landline. "Hang in there, Joey. You're going to be all right. I'll take care of everything."

As Joey put his back head down, I marched over to the office, determined to do whatever I had to in order to get my keys and phone. A sound from inside stopped me before I could do anything. From inside the office, I would have expected screaming or cursing or things being tossed around. I heard none of that. What I did hear was what sounded like someone using the computer. The e-nerd was typing.

Joey was dying and the e-nerd was typing!

My body grew hot with rage and I pushed on the door; it wouldn't open. I pounded away; the lock held. I had found the one thing Haradakis had not skimped on.

Joey started to cough, a thick, wet cough, as the typing went on.

Frantically, I looked around for something to bash down the door with. My hunt stopped when I spied a fire extinguisher. Ripping it off the wall, I used it as a battering ram, furiously pounding away at the door. It splintered then broke completely. I kicked the remaining pieces away then entered the office.

I thought I was ready for anything, but I wasn't ready for what I found: the e-nerd was sitting at the computer, body slumped backwards in the chair with no visible sign of life. Even so, I approached cautiously, but he didn't move at all. I glanced over his shoulder at the computer screen, to see that he seemed to be typing a blog.

I scrolled to the top and read it.

Binder's Blog: I'm not alive. The heart attack killed me, but I was able to inject myself with the first dose of the serum as I died. It brought me back to some semblance of life, but the Next project was wrong; this isn't living, this is hell on Earth. My memory is going, long term first then short. Right now, I can't remember where I grew up and even the memory of my parents is fading.

With the administration of the second and third doses, I doubt I will get any better, but I have to try. The survival instinct is too strong even though I know that, should this fail, I will become a creature devoid of any intelligence other than the will to survive and carrying around a virus with a one hundred percent mortality rate for anyone I infect.

As I found out too late, that's what Next wanted: a living corpse capable of killing everything in its way. Think of the military implications of something like that.

I can't get back at Next for my rebirth; they're too well insulated for that, but someone is going to pay for my death and I know who it is.

Before I died, I analyzed those Appeal Meals and found they contain an enzyme that preys on weak-willed people like me, making it impossible for us to stop eating the crap they serve. You eat one then, try as you might otherwise, you just have to have a second, then a third. I put on well over a hundred pounds in the last year and ate myself to death, but it wasn't my fault.

It was them! They murdered me and in my demise I'm going to massacre them.

And when I kill, you'd better believe they're going to stay dead.

Although the blog ended there, the writing continued. There were letters that formed paragraphs and what looked to be sentences, but they were all jumbled and didn't make any sense. This must have been what I had heard him typing through the door. Why? No time for that now. I had Joey to think of.

But the cell wasn't on the table. My heart sank as I found it laying in pieces on the floor under the e-nerd's foot. Quickly, I picked up the land line and put it to my ear. There was no dial tone. My eyes traced the cord to discover it ripped from the wall in a way I knew I couldn't fix.

Keys.

Where were my car keys?

I looked around and saw them in the e-nerd's hand. Taking a deep breath, I slowly pulled them free. As I did, his body moved and I screamed. I stopped when I realized he was still dead, my taking the keys having caused his body to fall to the ground. Sighing in relief, I hurried out of there to find Joey sitting at the table and staring into nothingness.

"Joey? It's me Stan."

His eyesight slowly cleared. "What did you find out, Stan?" His voice was low and weak.

I shrugged. "Nothing," I lied. *One hundred percent mortality rate.* "How are you doing?"

"Not good. The burning stopped, but I'm having trouble breathing and I've lost feeling in most of my body. And I'm starting to forget things, too," he said, his eyes looking at me sadly. "I'm dead, Stan, that guy killed me."

"Don't talk like that. I'll get you help."

"It's too late," Joey said, and laid his head on the table. I was afraid he was dead, but then he coughed that deep, vicious cough.

I had no doubt he was dying.

I put my arm around Joey, holding him as he shook. He was cold, colder than a living person should be. I sat down next to him and an uncomfortable feeling in my backside gave me the answer.

From my back pocket, I pulled out the golden case I had put there earlier. This must have been the stuff I read about in Binder's blog. If it worked for the e-nerd, it should work for Joey.

He would live.

But at what cost?

As Joey's coughing continued, I made up my mind. Taking a deep breath, I opened the case, the last two syringes starting to glow as I did. I took one out, gazing at the swirling emerald liquid.

And that's when the e-nerd staggered out of the office.

"Mine!" he roared and pointed at the syringe. His action startled me and I dropped the glass needle, breaking it. Its emerald contents puddled on the floor then began to bubble and steam. Shrieking wildly, the e-nerd dove onto the ground and licked it up, glass and all. When he had finished, he got up from the floor, wiping his own blood away with his sleeve.

Binder's head turned toward me, his gaze no longer glazed over. "Get out before I kill you, too," he said, lisping slightly as blood flowed from his mouth.

"I have to save my friend," I said.

"It's too late. Didn't you read my blog?" he asked then squeezed his eyes shut, hands shooting up to his head.

"But Joey is—"

Binder's hands pulled away from his face and I saw no further sign of intelligence. Snarling, he rushed toward me headfirst. This time I was ready. I leaped aside and he slammed into a wall, the impact accompanied by a nasty, squishing sound. This would have left him unconscious if he wasn't already dead. Instead, he just tottered a bit, then turned to face me with his head half caved in.

"Mine." He pointed at the NEXT case, then, going on what seemed to be instinct, began to shamble forward with his hands held out in front of him. "Mine!"

That's when I lost it.

Grasping the golden case tightly, I turned and raced out to my car. I jumped in, started it up and pealed out, leaving a strip of rubber behind me. In my rearview mirror, I saw the e-nerd shambling after me, or rather after the needle in the case I had put back in my pocket.

As I continued to floor the gas, the e-nerd disappeared from view and my relief grew. But so did my dread . . . and my guilt. I had left my best friend. I had left the person who had sacrificed his life for mine, lying near death and at the mercy of the thing that had killed him.

What kind of friend was I to skip out on Joey like that? What kind of human being was I? Muttering to myself, I brought the car around one hundred and eighty degrees and buried the needle.

The e-nerd was just returning to the restaurant as I arrived. He turned at the sound of the car and came running towards me, waving his hands and screeching incoherently.

Without a second thought, I plowed into him. There was a scream before the impact, and then his body just kind of exploded in a big green blast. I hit the brakes hard and the car spun around before finally coming to a halt. Quickly regaining my balance, I jumped out, the case now in my hand.

"Mine," a voice from nearby called. I turned to see what was left of the e-nerd's head and upper torso crawling towards me. "Mine . . ."

"Die!" I yelled, then raced forward and kicked at him with all my might. Again and again, my foot lashed out against what was left of Binder, bits and pieces of what was formerly a man flying away as I did. I kept going until he lay quiet in front of the restaurant. Quickly regaining my breath and senses, I raced inside, holding the precious needle in front of me.

Joey was exactly where I had left him and looking worse than ever. He was staring my way, but I could tell he only half saw me.

"Tell me again about the dream, Stan," he managed to whisper, his enormous frame now barely moving at all. "Tell it to me good."

I sighed, trying hard not to let him see the tears in my eyes. Joey had always liked to hear about our plan for the future when he didn't want to concentrate on other things. That was okay *this time*.

"It's like this," I began, keeping my voice as steady as I could, "as soon as we save enough money and I graduate college, we're going to open our own restaurant. It won't be a crummy little franchise like this dump. It'll be a real restaurant, a nice place where people can sit down and enjoy a good meal. It's going to be big, biggest restaurant you've ever laid eyes on and the most beautiful, too."

"And we're going to be the bosses, right?" he asked.

"Right," I said, and he smiled.

"Thanks, Stan, that's all I wanted to hear," Joey said. "You're a good friend."

And, still smiling, he was gone.

Tears flowing down my face, I took out the golden case and looked from the needle to my best friend who would never live to see our dream come true.

He had died saving my worthless life, but he didn't have to stay dead, did he?

Once more I looked down at his peaceful face, then took out the needle and brought it to his arm. Soon he and our dream would be alive again. I drew back my thumb and . . .

There was an explosion outside and bits of green goo hit the restaurant window. Although most of it was soup, a portion of it was recognizable. It was the bottom half of Binder's face and I could have sworn it was still mouthing the word "mine."

Yes, Joey could be alive again, but could I call what Binder had been *living?*

That's when I saw that the liquid in the syringe was starting to lose its glow. I had to make my choice and make it now.

Damned if you don't, and damned if you do.

I sighed and, knowing that whatever I did would be wrong, made my decision.

Better Living Through Chemistry

by

Becca Morgan

The day started out normal enough. Dakota Eyre was being his normal self, making a joke at anything that moved. His dark brown hair was in his face in that style that every "cool kid" has. His hoodie could hold a freaking elephant. Seriously, what's the point of that?

All the girls were either staring at Coda and giggling, or staring at me.

It's a new thing that girls look at me, Gregor Blackwood. Me, in my trench coat, tight dark blue jeans, and combat boots. Me, who has been compared to Adam Gontier, the lead singer on Three Days Grace, which is one of my favorite bands. Me, who is referred to as the vampire or zombie goth-boy. Me, who is skinny and pale with black hair in, sadly, the "cool kid" style that every guy has, and grey eyes when I don't have blood-red contacts in them. Thing is, if the other guys notice the girls staring at me, I get shoved into a locker until my only friend, Coda, comes and lets me out. Anyway, back to school.

Mrs. Evans was really strict today. She had been for the last couple of days, and no one knew why because she was our nicest teacher. She kept assigning homework over and over. There was even a rumor that she had been in the nurse's office before our class.

"Mr. Knapp!" she said.

Next to me, Mike jumped; he had been chewing gum, which didn't used to be a big no-no.

Mike went up to the front of the class, spit out his gum into the trashcan, and started to walk back to his seat. Mrs. Evans grabbed his arm. Mike yelped and the class went silent.

Mike finally managed to say, "Yes, Mrs. Evans?"

Then all heck broke loose.

I've seen teachers get mad, but not to bite a person. Mrs. Evans ripped a big chunk of meat from Mike's neck. Mike screamed. Everyone, except me, screamed. Blood sprayed everywhere.

"Yummy, yum, yum," I said in my normal "I don't care" voice. "Human flesh is *so* tasty." I got horrified looks.

Mrs. Evans stopped eating Mike and looked up at the rest of us.

"OMJ!" (Oh my Jonas, I think, but if I was wrong, I wouldn't care) some girl in our class screamed. "What do we do? What do we do?"

I sighed; people like that give us freshmen (in Mike's case, a *fleshman*) a bad name.

Mrs. Evans lurched toward Coda. He glanced at me, so I tapped my head. Dakota got a "what?" expression, but before I could explain, Mrs. Evans tackled him.

I jumped up. The classroom was crazy. Some people surrounded Mike, whose blood was still gushing out. Everyone was screaming their heads off. Coda was on the floor, trying to hold Mrs. Evans as far away from him as he could. Her teeth snapped at his face.

"Didn't know this was what your detention was for," I said as I dropped down beside Coda.

"Gregor! Get her off me already!" Dakota said.

I grabbed the back of Mrs. Evans's shirt and pulled. When I felt how cold she was, I knew for sure.

"You have to bash her in the head, you retard!" I yelled.

Together we got the teacher off him and shoved her away. I threw Coda the nearest copy of someone's algebra book.

Dakota looked at the book, then at me. "This isn't one of your horror movies! This is real life!"

"The teacher just ripped Mike's throat out and tried to eat you," I said.

The whole class watched as Dakota took the book and went toward Mrs. Evans. They couldn't believe it. They even stopped screaming to stare.

Mrs. Evans's face was very sorrowful, but she was dead, so she had a reason. Coda slammed the book into her forehead. Blood splashed on him. He kept hitting her until she stopped moving.

The class was silent. Dakota dropped the book and stepped back, looking at the blood on him.

"Well," I said, "you just ruined a perfectly good textbook. They'll probably make you pay for it."

The rest of the class ran out of the room, probably to go home and get away. We could hear more screams from all over the school. That was when I realized it might not be just Mrs. Evans. I started looking around for a good weapon. Something better than an algebra book. Dakota stayed standing there, staring at the dead teacher.

Three older kids ran into our room. One was Edgar "Skullcrusher" Thompson, the quarterback on the football team. Ed wore his letterman jacket, his hat and jeans. He had a baseball bat in each hand. The next was Mandy Reines, a rich attention hog with creepy blonde hair and creepier matching outfits. Every guy, except little old me, was in love with her. I didn't see why. But I knew that she hated me for not liking her. Whatever, and people call me the freak. Last came Tux Man, Jake Sittuar, who was known for always wearing a tux jacket over a tucked-in button-up shirt, jeans and dress shoes.

"The teachers are eating everyone!" Mandy squealed.

I sighed. She and Jake were seniors, but she acted like a middle schooler, while Jake acted like he was thirty.

"Really?" I said. I was trying to sound amazed, but failed miserably at it. "Hey, Ed, where did you get the bats?"

"The gym. Duh," Skullcrusher said.

"I thought you had . . . oh, never mind," Dakota said. We all knew that Edgar skipped most of his regular classes to hang out in the gym.

"Well," Jake said, in a voice that was all formal and polite, "we going to, as you kids say, 'Pop this joint'?"

"Yeah, but, dude," Dakota said, taking a bat from Edgar. "Don't try to talk like us. It's wrong."

"Yes! It's working! Mwhoo hoo ha ha ha!" Milton Thidwick said. "My days of listening to my parents are over!"

"That's great, Milton," Sarah said. "But it's not just your parents. It's everybody's parents. And grandparents. And everybody. Me and Dash had to fight through a bunch of zombies just to get to your house."

Milton turned from his Machine and pushed up his goggles onto his forehead to look at them. Sarah's hair, normally light brown and angelic, was covered in blood. She held a large fire axe good and tight. Dash, whose blackish-red hair might also have been covered in blood but it was hard to tell, had a flamethrower. They, like Milton, were twelve.

"But it was a great plan," Milton said, tugging at his lab coat. "No more rules. I got rid of all the grownups! Everyone over eighteen!"

Sarah gave him a glare. "And my dog. My dog died."

"He did? Buster?"

"Well, Buster *was* over eighteen," Dash said.

"Milton Mortimer Thidwick, you killed my dog!"

"Sorry," Milton said.

"And come on, Sarah," Dash said. "This was your idea."

"What! I said it would be nice to have no rules and no parents, not to turn every adult in America into flesh-eating zombies." She pointed at Milton. "You could have made something else. But no, you just used chemicals to do your job. *Again!*"

"Gotta say, though, the effects are awesome," Dash said. "Good job, Milt!" They high-fived.

Sarah smacked her head. "What happens when *we* turn eighteen, then?"

"Dude. That's ages away. I need some chips." Dash headed for the kitchen.

Milton sat next to Sarah and took off his goggles. "I really am sorry about Buster."

Sarah started crying. "You always kill my ideas, Milton," she said, sobbing. She leaned against him. "You ruined people's lives. You have to stop the chemicals."

"But that would to destroy the device, and that could kill everyone in town, grownups *and* kids," he said.

"It's too late anyway." She stopped crying and stared into Milton's green eyes. "Even if the zombies don't get us, how can we survive? It'll be hard, harder than it was with parents. You've doomed us all."

She stood up and started to walk out of the room.

"Harder?" Milton asked. "How? All the grownups are gone!"

Without turning, Sarah said, "You've ended America. Not destroyed, but it will become that. It's the end of the world. Did you think it would be easy?" As she walked out of the lab, Dash came back carrying a bag of chips. "Come on, Dash, we're leaving."

"Why?" he said, his mouth full.

"Because that chemistry geek needs to think about what he's done."

Wow. That's all I have to say about the hallway, wow.

School had never been like this.

Teachers were limping around, chasing or eating students. Blood and guts were everywhere. Edgar had to cover Mandy's mouth just to stop her from screaming every single time we saw a dead body.

Somehow, we managed to pass all the zombie teachers without being eaten. That really impressed me. Outside, there was a severed hand lying on the ground. The zombies were gone, though. I picked up the hand, right after Edgar had removed *his* hand from Mandy's mouth, and I held it next to her face. Of course, she screeched and started doing the severed hand dance, which was a lot like the bug dance.

"Gregor," Jake said, frowning and looking disgusted. "This is no time to be playing with leftover body parts."

"Fine," I said and threw the hand at Jake.

Do you know how funny it was to see a teenager in a tux do the bug/severed hand dance? It's the best thing ever. I even started laughing, something I hardly ever do.

"So hey, Mr. Vampire Guy," Edgar said, which sounded wrong on so many levels. "Why are the teachers eating people? 'Cause if you don't answer, I'm blaming you for the whole thing."

Now everyone was staring at me, like they really did expect me to know. I guess they probably did. I am the one always reading about zombies, horror and other fun stuff like that.

"Hey, this wasn't *my* idea," I said. "If I was going to start a zombie horde, I wouldn't start with the teachers."

"That is true," Dakota said. They all looked at him. "What? He's gone over it with me thousands of times."

"Oh yeah, and that's not creepy at all," Jake said. "Moving on. How do we stop these things?"

I was about to say something when a tall guy in a Pokémon shirt and cargo pants came running up to us. He had a gun in one hand and was holding a kindergartener in his other arm. Me and Dakota almost attacked him before we realized he wasn't a zombie and the kid wasn't a snack.

Then Edgar pushed past us. "Clay!"

"Eddie!" The kindergartener, Edgar's little brother, scrambled down and jumped into Edgar's arms.

"Uh," Coda said, "who's the guy with the gun?"

"I'm Bobby," the guy in the Pokémon shirt said. "This my gun. I getted it from the dead-police-guy who tried to eat us."

Edgar set Clay down and held out his hand for the gun. "Gun. Now."

Bobby moved the gun to his side and said, "No! No, no, no, no! I founded it! It mine! Mine, mine, mine! It go pew pew pew pew!"

"What the f—" Dakota began before Edgar glared with a not-in-front-of-my-little-brother glare.

"—freak," Coda finished.

A groan came from the side of the building. More zombies shuffled around the corner. I saw our mailman, a lady I recognized from the grocery store, a dude in a suit, and then I stopped counting.

"Let's go," I said.

"Where?" Mandy asked.

"Jake's."

"What?" Jake jumped in front of me. "You know you weirdos aren't allowed at my house. My father—"

"Is probably dead like every other adult. Now let's move!" I gave Jake a shove. We go way back, if you can call it that. He and his friends were the ones who started pushing me into lockers and throwing my shoes on the roof when I was about the same age as Edgar's little brother.

"Hey," Coda said. "That guy's an adult." He jerked his thumb at Bobby, then looked again at the Pokémon shirt, and added, "I . . . uh . . . I guess."

"I'm in first grade," Bobby said proudly.

Edgar leaned over and kind of whispered at us. "He got shot in the head or something when he was in the army. Messed up his brain. He's, like, six. Like, forever."

"Can't we just go already?" Mandy jingled her keys. "My car is right over there. Hurry up!"

"Sarah? Dash? Mom? Dad? Anyone living?"

Milton wandered through the house, not finding anyone.

"Hello? Someone answer me!"

In the kitchen, his mother's purse lay on the counter, its contents spilled out. The back door was open. There was blood on the floor, and bloody footprints led onto the porch.

There was groaning outside.

He didn't even want to look. He just shut the door and locked it. Then he went back to his lab. The Machine was still going. It bleeped and it blooped. Lights flickered. The vents hummed. Inside, chemicals bubbled. Wisps of green steam came out. He looked up through the skylight and saw the pipe leading outside, still shooting out a big plume of green smoke.

Sarah wanted him to turn it off.

Turn off his Machine!

After he worked so hard!

And it was too late anyway. The chemical formula was already in the atmosphere. It was circulating all around the world. Even if he turned it off now—*if* he could turn it off without having it explode and leave a crater where the town used to be—the reaction wouldn't stop.

He sat on the sofa, and that made him cry. It was the sofa where his friends sat when he was working. The sofa where his mother and father sat when he was showing them something. The sofa where he had lost his best friends.

The sofa where he sat, crying, continuing to call out for his friends and parents.

We crashed the car.

Well, Mandy crashed the car. Mandy, it turned out, only barely passed her driver's test. That was when she wasn't freaked out and trying not to run over zombies.

When we ran into the wall, Edgar swore like a sailor, Dakota only swore once but loudly, Mandy screamed, Jake grabbed at the side of the car, Clay and Bobby both whimpered, and I, being great and all powerful, said, "Well, anyone want some food while we're parked?" Groans of mental pain came from the high schoolers.

We managed to pull ourselves out of the car. Lucky for us, the brick wall was in front of the perfect place, a hunting shop, named Guns 'n' Stuff.

Guns 'n' Stuff. Sometimes I love this town. I went up to the storefront and peered in.

"This is no time to be window-shopping, Gregory," Jake said from behind me.

I flipped him off as I opened the door to the shop. It creaked outward and a zombie fell on me, knocking me down. I landed on the sidewalk with this cold, greasy, heavy, stinky chunk of meat on top of me. Crazy Old Brian, the owner of Guns 'n' Stuff. He was trying to eat me.

As I struggled with him, I heard the others shouting but nobody was being much of a help.

A gunshot rang out.

Crazy Old Brian's head got a big hole in it and I was splashed with gunky cold blood and lumps of brains like thick oatmeal and jelly. The smell got worse. Unbearable. But he stopped moving. Headshot. Just like it was supposed to work.

I pushed the body off and got up. Bobby stood there with the gun. He grinned at me. I grinned back. For a second, I thought of licking the blood off my lip. Mandy was already pointing at me and doing the icky blood dance. It was a lot like the bug dance and the severed hand dance.

But it really smelled bad, and I figured it'd taste even worse. I wiped my face with my sleeve.

We went inside and started looking for weapons. Dakota went right for a shotgun, broke into the glass case, and grabbed some ammo as well. I went over and smacked the boxes out of his hands.

"Dude!" he yelled, getting everyone's attention. "What was that for?"

I glared at him. I'm nice to my only friend, aren't I? "Can you *use* a gun? Can anyone in here besides Bobby the Barbarian use a gun?"

"Ah, yes," Jake said raising his hand. "My dearest father is a huntsman and took me . . ." He trailed off as I stared at him.

"No one asked, Tux Man. And no one cares," I said. "Get a gun."

Edgar handed a gun to Jake and everyone else put their guns down to pick up the "stuff" half of Guns 'n' Stuff. Hatchets, batons, tasers, knives.

I handed Bobby the shotgun and he smiled and set the pistol down. I pocketed it while no one was looking. We continued gathering weapons for a few minutes.

"We're wasting time," I whispered to Mandy, who was next to me.

"Do you think it's a good idea to go on foot to Jake's house from here?" She pulled me over to an area of the shop where the others weren't. "You're the expert here, Gregor. Walking past the firehouse and police station *can't* be a good idea."

I sighed. I've known Mandy for as long as I've known Coda, almost my whole life. My mom and her dad even dated for a while, which made it weird the one time she asked me out. I said no. Mandy didn't take that so well. I, as it turned out, was the only guy that had said no to going out with her.

"We don't have to go to Jake's anymore," I said as Mandy lifted up a set of stupid girly throwing stars in a pink case. I quickly took them from her and put them back. I gave her a big honkin' machete. "We just need to get out of here soon. We're making a lot of noise and zombies still have their ears unless they were cut off."

Mandy made a face at the last part, but managed to whisper back, "Well, it seems like you're in charge, because Mr. King-of-the-School is too busy looking at guns."

Jake was voted King of the School because he was popular, had money, and bribed the entire school. I looked over at him. He was scanning different guns like he was shopping for a new car.

"Me? In charge?" I put my hand on her forehead. "Are you feeling okay? Don't zombie-out on us."

She looked at me and I realized I was touching her. I removed my hand from her forehead in a hurry.

"Okay, my group of losers." I stood in the center of the shop to get their attention. "We're heading to my house."

"Why? Who put you in charge?" Jake said.

"You got a better idea? Let's hear it."

He just stared at me, and we all knew he didn't have a better idea.

"Actually, we have three choices," I said, turning to everyone else. "We could go to my house and get the key to my Z-Shelter."

Dakota smacked his head. "Dude, please, not the Z-Shelter stuff again. That place creeps me out."

"We could hide out in Coda's junkyard fort," I continued, "or we could find out what is actually happening."

Mandy raised her hand. "Um?"

"What?" I asked, annoyed.

"Do you think maybe—this is crazy—but maybe it might have something to do with that cloud of green smog? You know, the one that's been floating around town the past couple of days?"

"Hey, yeah," Edgar said. "That's about when all the grownups started getting weird, isn't it? I thought that was from a factory or something."

"There's no factory in town," Coda said. "It's just coming from that geeky homeschooled kid's house."

"Hang on," I said. "What geeky homeschooled kid?"

"The one who's friends with that creepy Masterson girl, and the kid who's always starting fires."

"The Thidwicks, Mastersons, and Petersons are well respected families and—" Jake said.

I punched him. Not in the gut like normal, but in the face. Guess I'd just had enough of his voice.

He stumbled back and grabbed his nose. For a few seconds everybody just looked at me, then at Jake, then at me again.

Edgar changed the subject. "I don't get why we have to go talk to people younger than us," he said. "They're like twelve or something. We can take care of ourselves."

"Good point, Skullcrusher," I said. "That makes as much sense as Jake and Mandy letting you follow them around and then letting me and Coda follow you around."

Edgar just looked at me. He's normally quiet when around anyone that isn't on the football team or the cheerleading squad. You wouldn't know it but he's actually pretty smart. He's one of the best students in school but asks all the teachers to treat him badly like any other dumb jock. "You win, Vampire-guy," he said.

"I'm going to go check out this green smog," I said. "If you guys want to come, you can. Even Loser-Tux-Man can come if he wants."

When I reached the end of the block, I turned to see who was following me. Mandy was the closest, then Dakota, Edgar, Clay, Bobby.

In the back, pretending he wasn't following, was Jake. I smiled and kept walking.

"Sar', you're mad, aren't you?" Dash asked. He was flipping through channels on the TV in Sarah's house. Breaking news. Zombies. News flash. Zombies. We interrupt your regularly scheduled programming for this zombie update. Zombies in your house, film at eleven.

"Me? Mad? What would give you that idea?" Sarah punched a wall, then buried her head in her hands and started crying.

Dash stood there for a while, thinking that he *should* hug her, but that would mean hugging a *girl*. Eew city. After a long time of Sarah crying, Dash finally embraced her. Quickly. Then let go.

"Milton was just being himself, Sar'. He can't stop that, 'cause, well, he's Milton," he said.

"A really freaky geek that uses chemistry for his job," she said. "That same Milton we became friends with back in preschool. Wasn't that an exciting day? Let's bring two really smart people and a pyromaniac kid together in the same room at the same time!"

Dash laughed, then paused. "Hey! I'm smart, too!"

"What's ten times twenty-five divided by two?"

"Uh . . ."

"Exactly."

"What's the correct amount of gunpowder to add to a firecracker?" he countered.

"How should I know that?"

"Because you're 'smart.'"

She sighed. "Why do I hang out with you?"

"Because we're both friends with Milt."

"Oh, right! Zombies! We have to do something! Let's go back!" She grabbed Dash's wrist and ran toward the door. "Maybe if we talk to him again, we can figure something out to—"

There was a knock on the door; they stopped short.

"They're here," Sarah whispered.

I kept pounding on the door.

"This *is* the Masterson Place, right?" I called over to Jake.

"It has to be!" Jake yelled as he hit a zombie with the butt of his gun.

The group fought zombies while I knocked on the door. How unfair was that? I've been waiting all my life for this and I got put in charge, so I had to knock on doors while they busted heads.

They all had horrified looks on their faces. These were their neighbors they were killing, and I guess for some reason it bugged them.

"Hey!" I pounded harder on the door. "We're out here fighting zombies and we want to talk to you about your nerd friend!"

The mail slot opened a bit and I crouched down to look in. Eyes stared out at me.

"What?" the eyes said.

"Can we come in? There's zombies out here."

The door opened and a couple kids were in the doorway. A black-haired boy and a light-brown-haired girl. I quickly stepped into the house and the others ran in after me. After we all got inside, the girl shut the door and we all looked at each other. Jake made introductions like we were at a fancy party, except his voice was stuffy because I may have broken his nose.

"So, what makes you bring the zombies to my house?" the girl, Sarah, asked.

"We want to know what's going on," I said, ignoring how Jake was about to go into a long explanation about it.

"Why would you think we know?" Dash said.

"Because you hang out with that geeky kid, and he's got weird green smoke coming from his house, and now there's zombies," I said.

"Yeah, and wasn't he the one who crashed that Town Hall meeting saying something about making parents pay for forcing their kids to do chores?" Edgar said.

"I remember that," Mandy said. "Wasn't he also the one who let a yogurt monster loose in the park?"

"So," I said. "How'd he do it? Voodoo? Necromancy? Old spellbook? Raising demons?"

"Milton doesn't know anything about magic!" Sarah said. She sounded all offended. "He's a *scientist!*"

"Okay . . ." I said. "You're saying it is his fault, though."

"Fine," Sarah said, rolling her eyes. "But he didn't *mean* it. I guess it started with me saying it would be nice to have no rules and no parents bossing us around all the time. And, being Milton, he was just trying to help. The chemicals he used were only supposed to hypnotize them or something, not turn them into zombies and make them go around eating people."

"The green smoke," Mandy said. "Told you so."

Sarah nodded. "He's got this machine—"

"You mean *Machine*," Dash said, so we could all hear the capital letter.

"And it's affecting anybody over eighteen," Sarah continued, giving Dash a look. Then her face went sad. "Animals, too."

"Except Bobby," Edgar said. "He's twenty-five."

"Brain damage," I said. "He's only about as smart as Dakota."

Dakota punched my shoulder.

"Sorry, I mean a six-year-old," I said, not really sorry. "So, all we have to do is shut down this Machine, right? Then everything goes back to normal?"

"What about the grownups?" Mandy asked. "Would they go back to normal? What about the people whose heads we smashed? Or the ones who got eaten?"

"We can worry about all that later. The Machine is the big problem right now," I said.

Sarah said, "Maybe even a bigger problem than that. Milton said it can't be turned off without maybe destroying the city."

"Yeah," Dash said, looking kind of excited. "He said it'd go *boooom!*" And he made big explodey-gestures with his hands.

Weirdo. I raised my eyebrow as everyone else's jaw dropped. "Well, let's go. We have to do something. We should at least talk to this nerd."

"Greg," Mandy said, running to catch up to me. I nodded to acknowledge her being there. "That house is past the college. Won't that be Zombie Land USA? Why are we walking?"

"Do you have a better idea?" I asked. "You wrecked your car, there's too many of us now to fit in it anyway, and—"

Just then we came to her house. Her dad was in the yard. Her *zombie* dad. Eating somebody's poodle. She nearly screamed, but got it back together, and I even took her hand to help hurry her by.

"That was my dad," she said, tears creeping into her voice.

"Yeah."

"He always hated that dog."

"Cool."

She sniffed, wiped her eyes and seemed to stuff it all down. "What are we going to do about Jake?"

I looked at her, surprised. "What?"

She did a big eye roll. "Today's his birthday, you know. His *birthday?*"

"What? You mean Jake's birthday is today? His eighteenth birthday?" Mandy nodded.

"Great," I said. "Guess we have to kill him."

"But he's still okay, isn't he? He's maybe been in a snottier-than-usual mood for the past couple days . . ."

"Like the teachers and everybody," I said.

There was a gate ahead of us. The college campus. Someone had closed and locked it. Zombie students tried to reach through, groaning at us, but couldn't get out. I could see the hill behind the campus. The house up there had green smoke coming out of the chimney, spreading into a cloud.

Milton frowned as he looked out his window. There were crowds of zombies gathered in front of his house, and more kept coming. It was like they were being drawn to the Machine, like it called them.

"Go away!" he said. "I was trying to make you all stop bothering me and leave me alone! Now it's worse than ever!"

"Crudpickles," Jake muttered.

We were at the bottom of the hill and could see the house. We could also see all the zombies between us and it. They kept trying to climb the hill, tripping up it, rolling down it.

"Crudpickles?" we all said.

"I don't want to know," I added. "What now? Fight our way through?"

"What do they want?" Mandy asked.

"They must be focused in on the device that changed them," Sarah said.

"The *Machine*," Dash corrected.

"Or they want revenge on the one who did this," she said, elbowing him to shut up. "We have to save Milton."

Mandy grabbed my hand again. She was scared. Almost crying. I sighed and actually hugged her, something I never did. Touching was over-rated. Sometimes I smacked people for it.

"So we charge in like suicide bombers and probably die," Edgar said. He had his little brother on him piggy-back style. Bobby was next to him.

"We could leave," Dakota said.

"And probably die later when the zombies get us," Edgar said.

"No, we should go in," Jake said. "We need to go in."

Something in his voice really creeped me out. It was different than the usual way his voice normally creeped me out. I looked at Mandy and she looked like she had noticed it, too.

Jake started moving forward, toward the house and the crowd of zombies. As he went, he dropped his gun.

"Dude," Dakota and Dash said together. "Are you nuts?"

"Quit it, Jake," I said, shoving him back. "Don't go zombie on us yet."

Edgar said a couple of words that would have gotten him in trouble at school. "His birthday. I forgot."

When I shoved him, Jake stopped moving. Then he turned around and punched me. In the face.

He never punched me before, not during any of the times he's bullied me. It surprised me more than it hurt. One of my teeth felt loose. I fell to the ground, grabbing my face.

Jake laughed, but then his eyes kind of rolled back into his head. He didn't fall over but swayed instead. Then he groaned. He came at me, reaching and groaning.

Everyone else stood there, stunned and scared. I pulled out the pistol I'd taken from Bobby. My hand shook as I pulled the trigger. It shook so bad I totally missed. I fired again. The bullet hit him in the shoulder and knocked him sideways. Blood flew out all over Mandy and she freaked. Jake kept coming for me. He grabbed the front of my trench coat. His mouth opened wide for a big bite.

I shoved the gun past his teeth and pulled the trigger again. There was a muffled bang and the back of Jake's head exploded.

I turned to the group. They were scared and shocked by what just happened, but even more shocked by the look of sorrow that was probably on my face. We stood there staring at each other, until more of the zombies noticed us.

"We ready to charge?" I finally said.

Milton was still at the window when he saw something going on at the edge of the yard.

It looked like a fight, a group of people trying to force their way uphill to the house. Kids and teenagers. Some with guns, some with baseball bats, a girl whacking away with a machete.

Sarah and Dash were in that group. His friends. His best friends. His only friends. They were trying to get to him.

They all charged into the crowd of zombies, fighting away. Then Milton saw his parents. They hobbled over to Sarah and Dash, and killed them.

Killed them. Killed his friends. They died. His parents killed them. All because of him.

The others that were in the group were dying, too. People he didn't know were dying trying to stop his plan. He must have done something wrong.

Milton ran to the lab then to the Machine. The Machine he worked so hard on. The Machine he was so proud of. The Machine that killed everyone close to him. It was still humming, the lights flashing, the green smoke coming out.

He scanned the controls and found the button he was looking for: the self-destruct. The big red button he was forced to add to his creation. Sarah always made him promise to add one to anything he made, in case something went wrong.

Something like destroying the whole world and everyone he knew.

He lifted up the glass box that protected the button.

Milton gave one last look outside. The zombies appeared to be the only things out there that were still moving.

He looked back down at the button, sighed, and said, "I've ended the lives of this town, my friends, and . . . myself."

He pressed the button.

THE DECAY OF UNKNOWN PARTICLES
by
MARK ONSPAUGH

Celia, there's a chance you will never receive this. If you are unable to, it will pass either to my brother Dex in Florida or my cousin John Bell in Munich.

If neither of them are able to receive it, then chances are everything is lost.

It's funny, in a way. Today's the day everything went to hell, but it actually started off as one of the best days of my life.

Of course, that's because I asked you the big question. I had planned to do it at a big romantic dinner at our favorite spot on the wharf, but you looked at me with those large blue eyes, the hair falling across your face as you smiled sleepily, and I caved.

"Marry me," I said, and I realized it wasn't a question, but a plea.

You giggled, your sleepiness and our tangle in the sheets making you think it was a joke. I looked at you again, and you knew I wasn't kidding. I brought out the jewelry box from beneath the underwear in my dresser drawer and your beautiful blue eyes grew wide.

It wasn't a big ring. I'm only a captain and substantial pay grades are a couple of rungs up the ladder.

You never said "yes," just covered me with kisses and sent me out the door whistling.

I guess that's the last time in my life I was really happy.

Celia . . . . Baby, I told you I worked at Lawrence Livermore Labs outside of Oakland. I'm sorry, baby, I lied. The truth is, I've been working at Site 64, which the U.S. Army has code-named "Ouroboros," after the mythological snake eating its own tail. Those of us a bit less pretentious, what the Army called "wise-asses," christened it "The Big

Worm." Others who took certain things way too seriously would sniff, push their thick glasses up the bridge of their nose, and inform me that Plato stated that Ouroboros was supposed to be a perfect, immortal creature.

Typical military hubris.

We're in a large complex underground beneath Fort Ord. The base above-ground was decommissioned back in the 90s, but Site 64 has continued on in secret. I am not ashamed to say I got the job from contacts through my dad and my Uncle Bill. The brass used me as an "LCD Liaison." LCD stands for Lowest Common Denominator. It meant that the brains here at Site 64 had to make sure I understood what was going on, and then put that into a report. The rationale was, if I understood, the brass probably would, too. Hey, I never pretended to be a genius, and I was perfectly happy to work a job where I wasn't in hostile territory and got home every night about dinner time. God bless the U.S. Army.

Our facility contained the most advanced hadron super collider in the world. The French-Swiss collider failed to yield evidence of a Higgs boson, the so-called "god particle," and the brass had been on our butts to get results before the Illinois collider went on-line in 2012.

Out of that deadline came two truths that the military should tattoo on the foreheads of every bird colonel and multi-star general: six months is not a lot of time and people get careless when you rush them.

I headed to the base that day feeling great. You were going to be my wife and life was going to be beautiful. I pulled into an abandoned carwash a quarter mile from the front gate of Ord and drove into the wash area. A switch box for the carwash contained a concealed optical scanner that read my retina pattern. An aperture large enough for my car slid open ahead, and I drove down into the parking structure for Site 64.

Doctor Hadley was agitated as usual when I arrived. He was a short man, barely five feet. He weighed next to nothing and had just a few strands of white hair combed over his shiny, bald head. He had thick glasses and large, white teeth. He kinda looked like a cross between a rabbit and Elmer Fudd.

"Morning, Doctor Hadley," I said, sipping the last of my coffee.

"It's time, Lewis. Are your people ready?"

My "people" consisted of a graph plotter and a file clerk. Hadley was nervous so he was being more of a pain than usual. I replied with my usual measure of reverence.

"They've been ready for days, Doc. Let's make that Worm dance!"

The Decay of Unknown Particles

Hadley winced. He always hated it when I talked casually about his baby. Screw him. In light of what happened, he's—well, I guess none of us are lucky, are we?

You know, Ce, in the hours since The Incident, I've been wishing I had just called in sick after you said "yes," baby. It wouldn't have changed any final outcomes, but it would have given us a few more precious hours together.

I've been looking at your picture as I record this, baby. Man, you're beautiful.

Ouroboros had performed perfectly in all the preliminary tests. We had launched our streams of bound quarks, or hadrons, in either direction and that had been successful.

Everyone, Hadley included, was sure the Big Worm would exceed expectations.

I guess it did, at that.

I digress here a moment, baby, to talk about what went wrong. If they are able to clean up the mess here, there may be inquiries, investigations. If there are, some are going to bring up the concept of sabotage, which is just nonsense. Everybody on this project is carefully screened. This is both for security and our safety. Someone who is either unbalanced or hostile would wreak havoc with the research. But the brass is probably going to say that somehow the religious nuts infiltrated a secret government installation because they were ticked off we were trying to find "the god particle."

Don't buy it. I know the people here, and everyone was excited to be involved in something that might change the course of human history.

(Man, I say something like that and the irony is just too much.)

Personally, I think it was a two-part problem. The main fault lay in the brass rushing to get Ouroboros built. You rush them, and even the best people tend to cut corners to make deadlines and budgets, and something vital somewhere suffers.

In this case, the shielding around the collision chamber.

No one in the military is going to admit that. I also have a feeling that any investigative committee is also going to find the brass blameless.

And so it goes.

The other problem was Ordinaries.

As I had said, Fort Ord itself was decommissioned some time ago. Members of Monterey's homeless population were always trying to crash on the base. Some of them were such regulars they took to calling themselves "Ord-inaries." It was up to the Ouroboros MPs to sweep the base and send the Ord-inaries off to less restricted pastures. I know it's not an easy gig because they had to perform said duties without revealing the existence of an underground facility beneath the abandoned base.

How many times had I seen their commander, Major Peary, grabbing a cig or chowing down on donuts in the mess hall when his people were supposed to be on a sweep? How many times was he flirting with that pretty new captain from Alabama?

What a tool.

We estimate there were seven Ord-inaries sleeping in the sun when we "woke the Worm."

Peary's staff now swears they did a sweep, and that Peary himself monitored the cameras giving a complete view of the base.

Yeah, right.

In light of everything, of course, Peary might be one of the lucky ones.

Hadley had fired up Ouroboros, and hadrons were sent in opposite directions to meet in the collision chamber at speeds some thought would excel the speed of light.

Of course, there were also those who said our collider would create a black hole that would swallow the Earth and surrounding planets, or that the resultant particle might tear a hole in the fabric of space and let *something* through. It was like all the hysteria back before the atomic bomb tests, panicked bleating that the explosion of such a device would ignite and burn off the atmosphere, killing all life instantly.

Scientists then had done the same as Hadley did now: calmly gone on with their research.

I don't know what kind of energy we unleashed that day. I mean, does it really matter?

As soon as the collision took place, a klaxon sounded, indicating a radiation leak in the collision chamber. Such an alarm was a classic case of closing the barn door after the horse was gone. The sensors couldn't even indicate where the leak had occurred. The contractor responsible for the substandard shielding had probably installed the sensors, too.

Hadley was miffed because there seemed to be no results at all to his grand experiment. This was the same complaint of the team working on the Swiss-French collider. I wonder now if there actually were results, but their rig was up to code and the resultant particle/energy had been absorbed and dissipated, undetected.

Hadley's boys were going over the data on the test, trying to coax more luminosity out of the Cray-Omegas that had recorded the hadron collision when there was a scream in the corridor.

I had run out into the corridor with Hadley and his techies to see what was wrong.

That pretty captain from Alabama was cowering in the corridor, and the object of her fear was Private Geeting, who most everyone called "Gopie" because he seemed like a cross between Gomer Pyle and Andy Griffith's son Opie. Gopie was a nice enough kid, big and rawboned, his skin almost orange with freckles, his hair a red thatch that never laid down. He had been given a mop and bucket and told to clean the corridors on the far side of the Worm. Gopie always took orders with good cheer and a big, goofy smile.

He wasn't smiling now.

Slack-jawed and drooling, he shambled down the corridor, dragging the wet mop behind him and leaving a trail like a giant snail might make.

Sergeant Mendoza bulled past us to give Gopie the D.I.'s version of a good old-fashioned butt-kicking.

"Geeting! What the Sam Hill you doin', boy?" Mendoza yelled.

Gopie stopped and stared at Mendoza as if he had never seen him before. He stared like he had never seen another *person* before.

Gopie swayed, and Mendoza moved in, his face about an inch from the private's.

"Did you hear me, you sorry sack of . . ."

Baby, at that moment, Gopie's eyes lit up. I don't mean figuratively, I mean they began to flicker like a dang jack-o-lantern. They began to grow brighter, and Mendoza hesitated.

That's when Gopie bit into Sergeant Mendoza's face, and tore away much of the man's nose and his upper lip.

Blood began to pour from Mendoza's face as he screamed, and Gopie answered with an unholy wail. He was chewing on the flesh he had torn off Mendoza, and his eyes were flickering even brighter. He backhanded Mendoza and the sergeant's head rocked back and hit the wall with a crack. Mendoza hit the ground, unconscious. Gopie fell to his knees and grabbed Mendoza's skull. He smashed it against the tiles until it cracked open like a coconut, and then he began to devour what was left of Mendoza's brain.

One of the techies puked, then, and the sound of that, so normal under the circumstances, roused the rest of us. I was reaching for my radio to call the MPs when Peary showed up, brandishing his sidearm like he was freaking Dirty Harry.

Peary pointed at Gopie's chest and fired. A hole appeared in Gopie's chest like a mouth had opened and the private was propelled back a dozen feet or more.

One of the medical personnel, a short guy named Saunders, ran over to Mendoza with a med kit. It was a pretty useless exercise: anyone could see Mendoza wouldn't be barking at any more non-coms. Not on Earth, anyway.

That's when a stream of blue-white light rushed out of Gopie's eye sockets and into the exposed brain of Mendoza. Mendoza's eyes opened, and now his eyes were flickering like Gopie's. Mendoza grabbed Saunders and bit deeply into his arm. Mendoza must have hit the brachial artery because blood spurted out of Saunder's arm like a fountain. As Saunders was screaming, Peary was already zeroing in on Mendoza's head.

I had a feeling then, baby, and although such hunches didn't happen often, I've learned to trust them. I told Peary not to shoot Mendoza in the head, not with so many of us near by. Peary told me to go screw myself, and it was all I could do to drag Hadley, a couple of techs and myself further back.

Peary sneered at me and aimed at Mendoza, who was standing up. He had chewed through much of Saunders's upper arm and was now trying to pull the freaking thing off. There was a sickening wet, tearing sound as the cartilage sheared, and the arm came loose. Saunders had gone white, and was either dead or close to it.

"Whoa," Peary said, "I didn't think he could do it."

It was just like Peary to hesitate for some perverse reason like that, but not because someone like me had warned him.

Peary fired, and Mendoza's head exploded in a shower of flesh and bone and fireworks. "Fireworks" is a lousy word, but there was a shower of sparks and a ball of fire emerged from his exploding skull. The fireball caught Peary and a couple of his staff and reduced them to piles of gray ash. Those between Peary and my group fell to the ground and were still.

Hadley and the techs wanted to help the fallen men, but I convinced them it was no time to play hero. Those men were lost.

I hurried them back to central ops. We entered and I closed and locked the door. Hadley thought I had lost my mind. I directed him to a series of monitors that covered the corridors paralleling the path of the

Worm. There, where Peary had gotten his, Gopie and the fallen men were rising. All had that creepy jack-o-lantern eye business going on.

Hadley saw this and went a little pale. For the first time since I joined Project Ouroboros three years ago, it seemed the doc had nothing to say.

I made an announcement over the PA system that everyone in the complex should lock their offices or quarters and stay put until receiving further instructions. I knew that everything that happened was automatically being sent on an encrypted feed to the top brass in the Pentagon. I wasn't going to do anything else without a directive from a superior. CYA, as we say.

My radio squawked twice, code that the caller didn't want to be overheard. I only had one real friend on duty at the Worm, and that was Captain Robert "Bobby-Ray" Rayburn. You met him once, Ce, a tall and lanky guy with a gap-toothed grin and jet black hair that looked like it had never made the acquaintance of a comb.

I moved over to a quiet corner while Hadley and his team were reviewing data.

"What's up, Bobby-Ray?"

"We got troubles, Lew," he said, his voice low.

"No duh, 'Einstein.' Are you in your quarters?"

"Nuh-uh. Topside."

I groaned. There was no smoking in the Worm, so Bobby-Ray and others who needed a nic-fix often snuck one topside out behind one of Ord's abandoned barracks buildings. It violated about twelve regs, but it was one of the facts of life at the Worm.

"Can you get back without tripping the alarm?" It was my duty to rat Bobby-Ray out, but in light of recent events, I couldn't think of anything more trivial than sneaking a cig while off-duty.

"Neg, bro, the Worm's locked up tight."

"Can you hang tight, Bobby-Ray? We've got a major sitch down here in the belly."

"I got news for you, cuz. You've got an even more major sitch topside."

"What's up?"

"Check your phone."

Use of private phones was strictly forbidden, especially during a test. I knew I might finish the day busted back to corporal, but Bobby-Ray was my best friend and wouldn't make such a request lightly.

I checked, and Hadley and the others were still bent over the monitors, talking in hushed tones.

I checked on the footage Bobby-Ray was streaming my way, and that's when I first got really worried.

There were several Ord-inaries on the parade field, and they all had flickering eyeballs.

Whatever we had unleashed, it had travelled right through our rush-to-get-it-in-on-time shielding and had irradiated several homeless civilians.

"Bobby-Ray, don't let them see you."

"No duh, bro, I'm not stupid."

"Are you strapped?"

"Yeah, I got my sidearm. Six rounds . . . no, five."

"How many Ord-inaries you got up there, Bobby-Ray?"

"Looks like six, and I'm a lousy shot as you well know, bro."

"Hang tight. I got to check some stuff out with the TB."

"Top Brass? Are you nuts? They'll put us both out in the freakin' Sahara."

"Relax. I'll tell them Peary ordered you to go on reconnaissance."

"He'll never lie for me."

"He's not a problem anymore."

"Peary's dead?" Bobby-Ray sounded like he wasn't sure whether to be amused or shocked. "What's going on down there, Lew?"

"Same as up there. Bobby-Ray, if you have to shoot, don't shoot them in the head unless you've got a good fifty feet between you."

"I told you, Lew, I ain't that good a shot."

"Bobby-Ray, you gotta hang tough. Lock yourself in one of the old barracks if need be. I . . . I should warn you those Ord-inaries are probably cannibals now."

"Canni—What did those eggheads do, Lew?"

"I'll get back to you. Stay safe."

I disconnected and put my cell in my pocket. I wished now I had called you, Ce. It would have been nice to hear your voice one last time. Instead, I walked over to Hadley's little brain trust.

"Doctor Hadley."

Hadley turned. His face was even more pale than in the corridor. His team looked equally shell-shocked.

"We have to contact the Pentagon, Doctor. Do you have something to report?"

"It's too soon to be definitive, Lewis, and it may take years."

"Doc, I've got news for you: whatever happened out in the corridor is going on topside."

Hadley's eyes widened. "There are more of these . . . afflicted above ground?"

"Yeah. I'm guessing our shielding was sub-par."

Hadley and his brain trust bent together and murmured in low voices. Finally, he looked up.

"We must capture and contain all the afflicted before they get out into the general population."

"And that sounds like a job for the big boys to implement. What do I tell them?"

"We're not sure. We think maybe we cracked an Ur-particle."

"Is that the same as a god particle?"

"No, Ur-particles are theorized to form a lattice between dimensions. This keeps various parallel universes separate but essentially in the same space."

"So you broke one?"

"Possibly."

"And this is important because . . ."

"Because we think something got through."

"Like what?"

"Something that seems to feed on brain energy. In fact, in reviewing the sequence of events in the corridor, we think this may be a being of energy that actually consumes the brain for its unique energy."

"That's all very *Star Trek*, Doc, but why did Gopie tear Mendoza's face off?"

"This creature is, shall we say, consumed with feeding. It leaves a dominant pattern in the brain for feeding. The creature feeds on living brains, so its hosts do, as well. They're just not as efficient about it because . . . well, because . . ."

"Because their brains are being devoured by this creature from Dimension X."

"It's worse than that, Lewis. Two of the things that define life are consumption of nutrients and reproduction. The creature is also converting some brains into nests for its young."

I looked at him in disbelief. "Just how do you know that?"

Hadley motioned me over to the video monitors.

"You were wise, one might say prescient, to advise Major Peary not to shoot Sergeant Mendoza in the head," Hadley said. "We played that sequence in slow motion after seeing the results of that fatal headshot. Take a look."

I watched as the slo-mo bullet crawled across the final three inches and entered Mendoza's forehead. His head expanded like a balloon and then burst apart. Gore and blackened fragments of skull continued on outward trajectories. However, there were several spheres of energy that headed directly for the living. Some entered the now-affected techs. The others dissipated.

"We think they're the energy equivalent of spores," Hadley said. "If the creature loses its host, it cleaves to these smaller forms and seeks out new hosts. Luckily you pulled us out of range."

"That's why you want to gather up the other 'afflicted,' as you call them?"

"Yes, but any team doing so is going to have to wear some sort of radiation suit impervious to the energy of these creatures."

"Will our suits do the job?"

"We won't know without some testing."

"That sounds like suicide."

"Not necessarily. We can put sensor pads inside an empty suit and hang it in the corridor. Someone can shoot one of the afflicted from a safe distance and we'll check the readings."

"Doc, why don't we just shoot the creatures in the corridor and topside and be done with it?"

"Because these beings are adapting, learning." He pointed to the screen again, and backed it up several frames. "Watch these last two 'spores.'"

I leaned in. As the other spheres dissipated, two joined together. Combined, they traveled almost twice as far as the others. They nearly reached our group before dissipating.

"We're afraid the simultaneous destruction of several of the afflicted would create a large number of these 'ultra-spores,' perhaps durable enough to reach a populated area."

My radio squawked twice.

"Go, Bobby-Ray."

"Some do-gooders from a local homeless shelter just showed up," he said.

"Bobby-Ray, you gotta get those people out of there."

"I tried. They said they have a duty to help the helpless."

"Do they know you have a gun?"

"I can't shoot a civilian, Lew!"

"Dang, Bobby-Ray, use your head! You scare them with your gun. Fire a shot in the air if you have to."

"Okay. Is anyone coming to help us?"

"Hang tough, buddy."

We switched one of the monitors and saw there were four people in the van. They were motioning to some of the Ord-inaries and apparently were either too blind or too stupid to notice their lost lambs had jack-o-lantern eyes.

Bobby-Ray ran in to chase them off, and one of the Ord-inaries seemed to come from out nowhere and grabbed a girl in the van. The Ord-inary, who looked like a gym teacher I had in high school, bit deep into the face of the girl. We saw her scream as he punctured her eye with his teeth, and then Bobby-Ray panicked and shot him. For a lousy shot he placed the round square in the Ord-inary's melon. The sucker exploded and Bobby-Ray and the kids in the van collapsed. Within minutes there were now ten of the things on the parade ground, including my old friend Bobby-Ray.

I sent a report to General David Vincent at the Pentagon, Ce. I had a feeling the brass were monitoring things because phones and radios became useless. All communication was via encrypted text messages.

I sent the following message: ARE YOU APPRISED?

Command answered: AFFIRM.

Me: ORDERS?

Command: SIT TIGHT.

Me: WE NEED A TEAM TOPSIDE AS WELL.

Command: ALL NEEDS BEING ADDRESSED. GO DARK.

"Go dark" means we stop communicating until Command breaks the silence.

Meanwhile, some people just refused to follow my orders, and now the corridors are filled with brain-eaters. That's what I call them. Doctor Hadley insists on calling them "Dimensional Interlopers" or "Anomalous Lifeforms." I'm happier with "The Brain-Eaters of Dimension X." Anyway, a lot of people are now among the undead, including that pretty lieutenant Peary was so ga-ga over. I guess now that she's missing most of her face and her torso is just one big hole, he might not find her so attractive. You never know with some people. She's having a hard time of it. She's dragging her intestines behind her and other disobedient brain-dead morons are stepping on them. Hard for a woman to make progress in this man's army. Sorry, Ce, it's been a long day and I make bad jokes to keep from crying.

I asked Hadley if the human hosts wouldn't just collapse once their brain was devoured. Get this: he and the techies think the creature reshapes itself into an energy analog of the host brain. Like a hologram or something. It wouldn't be enough for the person to talk or drive a car, although Hadley thinks there might be further adaptation, a sort of learning curve. One day the hosts might seem just like human beings.

Except for the glowing eyes and being dead and eating brains, of course.

Oh, and you might be wondering if only human brains would do. We saw Bobby-Ray attack and devour a dog, so that answers that question. I guess Bobby-Ray would be embarrassed that he's the one we saw eating doggie brains, but what choice did he have? I thought it showed initiative. Sorry, Ce, getting a bit punchy.

Man, I don't want to spend eternity with some electrical hologram brain making me eat people and pets, the inside of my skull all scorched and my mouth full of raw flesh.

We've been stuck in central ops for six hours, wondering when we'll be rescued. Luckily we had a bathroom; I'm sure some of the offices have become very unpleasant, even without brain-eaters. I'm a little light-headed, all we've had between the five of us was a couple of stale fig newtons and half a baloney sandwich. You know I get loopy when my blood sugar drops, baby. Anyway, it's given me enough time to record all this. Hadley kept wanting to throw his two cents in but I told him to make his own G-D report.

LCD, baby, as in Love Celia to Death.

Now I just want to . . .

Wait . . . . There's a rumbling. Those morons are bombing the place!

The monitor screens all go to static as the entire installation shakes. The Worm is really dancing now!

Celia, the whole place is filling with light! Brightly dancing spheres in electric blues and butter yellows.

I want to run, but where?

Ce, please remember I . . .

It's in my head! In my . . .

[UNINTELLIGIBLE]

Oh! It's beautiful! Just beauti—

BLOOD, SPIT AND ASPARTAME
by
ADAM J. WHITLATCH

They say the road to Hell is paved with good intentions. Well, if that's true, then young Craig Vincent paved his own private path to the devil's front door when he set out on his mission to develop the perfect zero-calorie artificial sweetener: a non-saccharide that didn't have any of the nasty side effects of others like the headaches, brain lesions, and possible lymphoma caused by aspartame. Saccharin had been shown to cause both weight gain and bladder cancer in lab rats; studies were deemed inconclusive, but Craig still wasn't convinced it was entirely safe. Then there was sorbitol; he'd given that up the day his ex-girlfriend told him the sugar substitute in his favorite breath mints was used as a laxative in the veterinary clinic where she was doing her internship.

Yuck.

Craig peered through his goggles at the bubbling green liquid swirling in the glass flask in front of him and adjusted the valve on the side of the antique Bunsen burner. He closed the throat holes ever-so-slightly, dropping the temperature of the flame. He watched as the flame changed from a deep purple to a bright, vibrant orange. He smiled as he made a note on his chipped wooden clipboard.

A droplet of water from the pipes above him splattered onto his notes, splotching the fresh ink. He scowled up at the pipes, mentally cursing the university for kicking him out and forcing him to work in the substandard conditions of his basement.

Misuse of university equipment, my eye, he thought with a sneer. He didn't do anything to the dean's daughter that she didn't willingly consent to.

Finally the liquid in the flask had thickened to the desired consistency and he transferred the viscous substance to three waiting Petri dishes, making sure to pour precisely the same amount in each. Once the flask was empty, he pulled three small vials from the fridge and placed a drop from the first vial into the first dish, one from the second into the second dish, and so on. He carefully labeled the dishes, not wanting to mix up which mixture was which before stirring them with individual sterilized glass rods.

He placed the dishes in the small dorm room beer fridge, right next to a bottle of Smirnoff, and paused a moment to stretch, feeling the bones in his sore back pop one by one. He glanced at his watch; it was getting close to eight o'clock.

"Well," he said, "those will need a few of hours to cool, and then" —he approached a shelf lined with wire cages, each cage containing one white fancy rat. He reached out and patted the front of a cage labeled ARCHIMEDES— "show time."

He waved to the inquisitive rat sniffing at his fingers then turned to leave, whistling a happy tune as he climbed the wooden stairs to the ground floor of his home. As he switched off the light in his makeshift laboratory he wondered which sounded better on his pizza, sauerkraut or anchovies. Oh heck, why not both?

Later that night, after dinner, a cheesy B-movie, and a severe bout of indigestion, Craig staggered down the creaky steps to his basement laboratory and anxiously opened the fridge. He smiled triumphantly as he lifted the chilled dishes out one by one, examining the solidified contents approvingly.

Carefully, he began to crush the solidified solutions with a spoon, pleased at how easily the mixtures crumbled into fine crystalline granules. He'd have to do something about that color though.

There was no way people would use green sweetener in their coffee or on their cereal. It was really a trivial matter, but one that would eventually need to be addressed. He remembered one Thanksgiving back home in Davenport when his father, a known prankster, had colored the gravy blue with food coloring. No one would touch the gravy except his father, grinning like the Cheshire cat the entire time.

Once the samples were sufficiently crushed up, Craig crossed the room to the row of cages lining the wall and brought three back to the workbench, the cages labeled ARCHIMEDES, PROMETHEUS and GEORGE respectively. He placed one sample in each of the cages, noting which rat got which mixture on his clipboard. Archimedes and Prometheus immediately began to devour the emerald granules, but Craig noticed that

George seemed more reluctant to partake, sniffing warily at the dish and rubbing his nose with his paws.

Craig pulled a small portable tape recorder from his pocket. "Subjects One and Two show no aversion to their individual mixtures, but George seems cautious. Perhaps an odor undetectable to humans?"

But then slowly, tentatively, George stuck his nose into the dish and began to eat heartily.

"Disregard," Craig said into the recorder with a smile.

The next morning, Craig stumbled down the stairs bleary-eyed and still suffering the aftereffects of the infernal sauerkraut and anchovy pizza. His dreams had been plagued by horrible images of carnivorous pickles and talking cats. What he needed was some good news. He needed results, something to show for his three years of work besides a trail of dead rats and shattered Petri dishes. But his shoulders slumped when he glanced at the cages. Prometheus was lying on his back, his jaw slack and eyes closed.

He swore, smacking the table with his palm and startling Archimedes, who was curled up in a ball beside his own dish, only a small amount of the sweetener sample remaining. Craig reached under the workbench to collect the small black leather bag containing his surgical kit, muttering under his breath, wondering what it could be this time, the kidneys or the heart? More than likely the kidneys. Certain forms of glycol could cause crystals to form in the kidneys, halting the body's ability to filter toxins, resulting in nephrotoxicity; a slow, albeit peaceful death.

"Brilliant," he muttered, running a hand through his disheveled hair. "I just invented antifreeze."

He picked up his recorder and pressed the RECORD button. "Saturday, September 27th, 8:59 A.M. Subject Two, Prometheus, dead. Apparent cause of death seems to be nephrotoxicity; will perform a necropsy to be sure. Subjects One and Three show no signs of—"

Just then, Archimedes began to shake on the floor of his cage, only a tremble at first, but rapidly developing into a violent convulsion. Craig's lip curled in revulsion as disgusting green foam began to bubble from the rat's mouth.

He raised the recorder again and said, "Subject One is having some kind of . . . *episode*; appears to be seizing and expelling green foam from the mouth."

Craig continued to watch—the recorder still rolling—and recoiled as Archimedes spasmed violently, his spine breaking with an audible *crack*. The rat gave a final shuddering squeak and became very still as thick blood began to ooze from every orifice.

"Whoa!" Craig wiped sweat from his upper lip with the back of the hand holding the recorder. "The ASPCA is not going to like this."

He clicked the recorder off and looked from one cage to the other, shaking his head despondently. The squeaking of an exercise wheel caught his attention and he looked over to the third cage where George ran contentedly on the blue metal wheel. Craig sighed, happy he had at least one healthy subject left to observe.

He turned to get on with the unpleasant albeit necessary task of performing postmortem examinations on the dead rats.

Craig wiped the sweat from his forehead with the back of his latex-gloved hand. He blinked, forcing his eyes to focus as he pushed aside Prometheus's intestines, probing the abdominal cavity until he found the right kidney. He sighed; the kidney was enlarged and badly bruised, a telltale sign of nephrotoxicity. He really didn't want to cut into the thing, already knowing full well what he would find, but for the sake of the experiment he had to be sure.

"Okay, here we go," he said, raising his bloody scalpel. "You still with me over there, George?"

At the end of the table, George clung upside down from the roof of his cage by his toes, moving in erratic circles.

"Just let me know if I'm boring you," Craig muttered, returning to the necropsy. "We wouldn't want that, now, would we?"

Craig pressed the tip of the scalpel into the enflamed tissue firmly, meanwhile narrating the procedure into the rolling tape recorder standing upright on the table to the right of the necropsy tray. Slowly, he cut down to the bottom of the kidney and turned the blade to widen the incision and expose the interior of the damaged organ. As he suspected, the interior tissue was red and littered with black clots. The inside of this kidney looked like it had been shredded.

"Kidney exhibits signs of severe trauma and clotting," he said, addressing the recorder. "Apparent cause of death appears to be nephrotoxicity. Surprise, surprise."

Craig shoved Prometheus's tray aside and reached for the one containing the gruesome carcass of Archimedes. As he drew the tray closer, the foul stench rising from the corpse overpowered him and he began to cough. The green foam around the rat's head had dried to a hard shimmering crust; Craig prodded it with his scalpel.

"Subject One, Archimedes," he dictated to the recorder. "Cause of death is . . . undetermined. Subject exhibits massive hemorrhaging from the ears, mouth, nose and rectum. Spine appears to be broken somewhere in the lower thoracic vertebrae due to severe seizure-like activity. I'm making my primary incision now . . ."

He sliced through the snow-white fur into the muscle below, splitting the sternum and exposing the lungs and heart, holding the cavity open with a pair of hemostatic clamps. He prodded the organs, peering closely at each in turn.

"What the—?" he whispered, raising the volume of his voice to address the recorder. "Examination of the internal organs shows severe trauma to all visible major organ systems—respiratory, circulatory and diges—"

THUMP!

The noise startled him, cutting his dictation off mid sentence. He looked over and saw George, who only moments ago had been dangling upside down from the roof of the cage, lying very still on his back on the floor. He pulled the cage closer, peering through the bars at the unmoving rodent.

"George?" he said.

The rat didn't budge.

Craig pulled a ballpoint pen from his breast pocket and threaded it through the cage bars, prodding George's body with the capped end. When this did not garner a response from the animal, he poked harder, hard enough the rock the rat's body back and forth. Again, it didn't move; George was dead.

"No," Craig said, continuing to prod the rat. "No, no, no! This can't be happening to me! Wake up!"

He threw the pen across the room and didn't even hear it clatter against a row of glass beakers over his own cursing. He pulled at his hair in two heaping handfuls as he paced the room.

"Three years," he groaned. "Three freakin' years and what have I got? *Rat poison!*"

He continued to mutter angrily to himself as he jerked open the refrigerator door and pulled out the bottle of vodka. He unscrewed the cap and threw it into a far corner of the basement. He raised the bottle to his lips and took a long pull of ice-cold booze. When he finally came up for air he grabbed an empty glass beaker and sat down at the worktable, shoving the two necropsy trays aside—the dissected remains of both rats falling to the floor in a clatter—and poured three fingers of booze into the beaker. He peered over the edge of the table at the carcasses on the floor and raised his beaker high into the air, the clear booze inside threatening to slosh over the rim.

"Well, boys," he said. "Here's mud in your ruptured eyeballs." To the rat: "Sorry 'bout that, Archimedes."

He placed the beaker to his lips and knocked the drink back in one large, painful gulp, then poured himself another.

Craig awoke several hours later to a strangely familiar sound. He just couldn't place where he heard it before. The sound reached through the alcohol-induced haze clouding his brain and tickled his temporal lobe. Slowly, it dawned on him: it was the sound of tiny teeth gnawing on metal. Sometimes the rats would gnaw on their cage bars when he forgot to feed them.

How long have I been out? he wondered as he raised his head an inch and forced one eye to open.

The gnawing continued steadily.

"Shut up!" he said. "I'll feed you in a minute!"

The gnawing ceased momentarily, but then resumed, louder and more persistent.

"For crying out loud! I said I'll feed you in a min—"

He opened his eyes and looked directly into the dull red eyes of George, who was gnawing incessantly on the horizontal bars of the cage separating the two of them. The rat had already removed the white paint from three of the bars, leaving the bare metal slick and glistening with blood and saliva.

"George?" he whispered, unsure if what he was seeing was real or not.

As Craig brought his face closer to the cage to get a better look at the animal he'd presumed to be dead, George's eyes narrowed and he began to bite at the bars with renewed vigor, his front paws jutting out through the wire, reaching for Craig's face.

"What . . . ?"

Craig reached for the cage door and George immediately stopped gnawing, following the human's hands with his eyes. Craig opened the door and slipped his hand through the narrow hole, reaching for the rat. As his fingers brushed the white fur on George's back, the rat whirled and lunged, sinking its long front teeth into the tender flesh between Craig's thumb and forefinger. He screamed and tried to pull his hand out of the cage, but George's jaws clamped down, keeping the hand trapped in the narrow opening.

Finally Craig gave a panicked tug and screamed as a sizable chunk of flesh tore away from his hand, George's teeth still clenched together. Craig slammed the door hard and watched in horror as George turned his attention to the ragged chunk of bloody flesh, devouring it. Craig cursed, clutching his damaged hand to his chest, unaware of the blood soaking into his T-shirt. He tasted bile and vodka in the back of his throat as George finished consuming the flesh and resumed his previous activity of gnawing at the cage bars.

Craig finally looked down at the tattered webbing of his hand and looked for something to wrap it in, finally settling for a torn section of his already-ruined shirt. He paused to pick up the overturned bottle of vodka, took a short swig, then poured the remainder onto his wound. He screamed through clenched teeth as the alcohol burned the exposed flesh. He crafted a makeshift bandage from the shirt and wound it tightly around his hand. He collapsed against the wall and stared at the devil rat trying to chew its way to freedom, yearning for another taste of his flesh, no doubt.

"Son of a—" he gasped. "What's going on here?"

He reached for the tape recorder still lying on the table and pressed the RECORD button. The machine clicked in noncompliance. He tried again until he realized he'd let the tape run out while he drank. He flipped the tape over awkwardly with his injured hand and pressed the RECORD button again; the recorder's red light blinked at him.

"Subject Three," he gasped into the microphone. "Subject Three, believed to have been dead now appears to have merely been in some deep state of catatonia. Subject seems to have undertaken a dramatic shift in behavior, now exhibiting severe aggression and . . . and . . . the little creep *bit* me!"

He looked down at the bloody rag covering the wound—which had now begun to throb—and decided he needed to go to the emergency room. He tried to stand, but the room began to spin and vertigo overtook him. He fell to the floor, grabbing the table for support, but only managed to knock over the beaker, sending it crashing to the floor in an explosion of glass. He was far too drunk to go anywhere, he realized, and he had already lost quite a bit of blood; there was no choice but to stay put until he sobered up enough to drive.

So he sat there, cursing the rat until the drink reclaimed him and he fell into a fitful slumber.

Craig awoke to the sound of a cage clattering to the floor. He immediately thought of George and pulled himself up to the table. The cage was still there, but on the left side was a ragged hole where the bars had been chewed through and bent outward; clumps of bloody fur clung to the jagged ends of wire. Craig panicked. Where was George?

Somewhere off to his left was the frantic squeaking of rats and he remembered the sound that woke him. He ran around the table to the shelf on the wall where he kept the specimen cages and saw one of the cages on the floor, the plastic base broken and separated from the wire bars. He followed the sound of the squeaking until he found George, bloody and ragged, wrestling with a black and white rat. Socrates. It took him a moment to realize George was actually taking large, tearing bites out of Socrates's abdomen, paying no attention to the damage his opponent was dealing to his face.

Craig reached into a nearby toolbox with his good hand and closed his fingers around the handle of a heavy wooden mallet. He hefted the mallet, testing the weight as he advanced on the two fighting rats, determined to bash George's brains in. Craig screamed as his legs flew out from under him and his vision exploded in a starburst of reds, blues, and greens as the back of his head smacked the cold concrete. Something wet coated the back of his head. Water? Blood? The idea that Socrates's water bottle had spilled onto the floor when the rat knocked over the cage drifted across his mind.

Slowly, the colors faded and everything turned black.

Someone tugged on his lip. At first the sensation was simply annoying, something to be batted at like a persistent housefly, but then it started to hurt. Suddenly the tugging sensation was replaced with wetness and for a moment Craig thought he was drooling, but then he tasted it: the coppery metallic taste of blood. He opened his eyes and found his vision filled with black, white and red fur.

What's black, white and red all over? he thought with a childish giggle.

He brushed his hand over his face and felt fur. His finger closed around a small furry body and he raised his head to look into the single red eye of George, the other side of his head nothing but an empty socket and bloody bone.

"Hi, George!" he cried gleefully.

He felt the tugging sensation on his lip again and looked down to see Socrates ripping pieces of his bottom lip off with his giant buck teeth.

"Go away!" he shouted, swatting the black and white rat away with his free hand.

A sharp pain in his bad hand brought his attention back to George, who was biting through the blood-soaked strip of cloth to get at the open wound.

"Why you biting me, George?" said Craig dreamily as he began to stroke the rat's stripped head with his forefinger. "I will hold him and love him and squeeze him, and call him George."

Suddenly Craig felt as though his chest was on fire; sharp stabbing pains tormented his left arm. He dropped the rat—which promptly went to work on his lips again—and clutched his arm. Deep in the back of his consciousness, the medical student in him was vaguely aware of what was happening, not that he could have done anything about it anyway. The last thing he saw before the world went dark again was Socrates and George sharing a picnic on his face.

The next morning Craig's mother, Mary, unlocked the front door with her spare key and called out as she kicked off her shoes.

"Craig, sweetie," she called. "Laundry day."

She wrinkled her nose as she stepped from the foyer into the living room. A foul odor hung in the air and her gag reflexes brought a tablespoon of that morning's breakfast to the back of her throat. She surveyed the room until her eyes fell on the remains of the anchovy and sauerkraut pizza, a few flies buzzing above its surface.

"Oh, Craig," she said. "I thought I brought you up better than that."

Suddenly, a loud thumping sound from behind startled her. She whirled around. Her hands clutched her chest. The basement door shook in its hinges as the thumping came again, this time harder and louder. She took a tentative step forward.

"Craig, sweetie," she said. "Is that you?"

The door thumped again and for a moment she thought about leaving and calling the police from the neighbor's house, but then she had a terrible vision of her baby boy, injured and unable to call out for help. Slowly, hesitantly, she reached out for the antique door knob. She turned it slowly.

She screamed as the door was forced open from the other side the instant the latch was slid back. She fell hard on her rear, tears welling up in her eyes as she bruised her tailbone. A low moaning caught her attention and she looked up at the ghastly monster standing in the doorway. There, in a torn and blood-stained T-shirt, his face and lips shredded by countless rat bites, was Craig. His eyes were a cloudy gray and vacant as those of a corpse.

Mary cringed. "C-Craig? Sweetheart?"

The ghoul that used to be Craig Vincent shifted his gaze to the cowering woman on the carpet and bared his teeth, an easy feat with his lips hanging in tatters. Mary held up her hands, but Craig was on her in an instant. She shrieked as his teeth sunk into the tender, wrinkled flesh of her throat. Her screams turned to blood-curdling gurgles as he tore away a long strip of flesh and chewed it slowly.

"Mmmm," he groaned, blood dribbling down his chin. "Sweet."

WALKING WITH THE DEAD

by

ANTHONY GIANGREGORIO

Richard Dearborn slowly opened his eyes and looked around the room.

It was bright white, the lights blinding him with the intensity of a supernova. He blinked a few times. Slowly, shapes came into focus.

Heads covered in white masks hovered over him with people yelling at one another.

Medical terms were being tossed around and in his foggy state he didn't understand what had happened to him. He tried to get up, but he couldn't move. His arms, neck and legs were strapped to something. A table?

He felt cold. No, wait, he was hot.

Odd.

It was like someone had placed an air-conditioner on his lower half and a heater on his upper half. He tried to move his head, but it wouldn't budge.

Talk, he thought. *I need to talk, tell these people I'm okay, that they don't have to fuss over me so much.*

He opened his mouth; only gargles came out. Then he coughed, blood shooting up from his mouth and falling back onto his face.

"I'm losing him!" a voice screamed from somewhere far away. Losing him? What did that mean? Was the voice talking about him? Was he dying? But how could that be? He tried to remember what he had done that day, but it was all a tangled mess.

Wait, I do remember, he thought. *I had been driving home from work. It had been a little before five and I had snuck out early when the boss was in another office chewing some poor slob out about the week's financial report.*

I took the Interstate home and then the off-ramp. I remember stopping at the local gas station for a pack of smokes and a gallon of milk. Susan had told me to get her some milk and some bread.

Oh great, I forgot the bread!

Maybe I could go out and get some later after I eat dinner.

So I left the gas station and then drove in the direction of that intersection everyone living in my city hated. It was a four-way intersection with a blinking red light in the middle that was about as good as that one bulb that always didn't work on the Christmas lights every year.

No one stopped at the four-way and it was always a free-for-all to get through it.

So I approached the intersection and . . .

And then it all goes blank.

"Give me a shot of adrenalin. Now, Nurse!" a voice screamed, but as his mind raced to remember what happened, Richard barely heard it.

Now what happened at that intersection that I can't remember? he thought.

Then he did remember and his breath caught in his throat.

He had waited at the intersection and when he thought he had a chance to go, he'd taken it, but there had been a cement truck coming way too fast on his left, and at the last instant, Richard realized the guy wasn't going to stop.

He was able to look out the driver's side window and see the man was talking on a cell phone and wasn't paying attention to where he was going.

In the flash, Richard remembered thinking it was the cigarettes he smoked that he thought were going to be the death of him, and not an overweight truck driver with too many cell minutes on his calling plan.

Then there was a crescendo of crashing glass and twisting metal and he was tossed across the car seat and pummeled by the air bag when it went off.

Nothing then; nothing but darkness.

Until now.

"I need the paddles now. Give me those paddles!" a voice screamed, the same one as before.

"Here, Doctor, take them. Ready when you are," a woman's voice said.

Was it Susan's? Was his wife here?

"Clear!" the doctor yelled.

Suddenly, Richard felt nothing but pain and his vision darkened as electricity shot through his body. His heart trip-hammered in his chest and he sucked in a breath, but then lost it.

There was a beeping sound coming from nearby, but then it went steady, like a low hum.

"He's not responding, Doctor." The woman's voice again.

"Up the juice. Let's hit 'im again!"

"But, Doctor . . ."

"Do as I say. I'm in charge in this trauma center, not you!"

"Yes, Doctor."

"Clear!" Voltage surged through Richard's limbs, feeling like acid coursing through his veins. "No, it's not working. His heart is too badly damaged!" the doctor yelled. "Nurse, get me the experimental drug!"

"What? But it's still in the trial stages. It hasn't even been tested on humans yet."

"I don't care. This man's dying and if I don't at least try then he's a goner. Do you want to tell his wife we didn't even try? She's right outside in the waiting room."

There was silence with the exception of people moving about. Then the nurse spoke again. "No, Doctor, I . . . I guess you're right."

Richard didn't know what was happening. He tried to talk but only garbled grunts came out.

Then he felt a piercing stab right where his heart was. There was a warmness that suffused his body as his heart pumped whatever the doctor had injected inside him.

"Okay, now give me the paddles again," the doctor said. "The juice on top of the drug should be enough to repair his heart."

"But, you don't know that," the nurse said.

"Listen, unless you know something about nanites, you need to keep your fool mouth shut and do as I say or I swear you'll be cleaning bedpans for the rest of the year by end of shift tonight. Do I make myself clear?"

"Yes, Doctor," the nurse replied, her answer now more confident.

"All right. Charge the paddles now!"

A whining sound filled the room.

"Clear!"

Richard's body jumped off the gurney and he felt a pain so great he thought he was going to die. The voltage shot through his heart. The drug coursed through his system. He gasped for air. Still semi-conscious, he heard the beeping stop and the fateful steady drone of its tone filled his ears.

It was the last sound he heard.

"Call it, Nurse: 6:22 P.M. I can't believe we lost him. I really thought he had a chance."

"It's not your fault, Doctor. He'd simply suffered too much trauma. There was really no chance," she said. "He looked like he'd gone through a meat grinder as it was."

The doctor tossed his bloody gloves on top of the table next to the corpse and shrugged out of his once-white lab coat, which was now a bright scarlet, as though tie-dyed.

"Well, I might as well go tell his wife," he said. "Have this room cleaned up and get the body to the morgue."

"Yes, Doctor. I'll see it's done immediately."

Nodding curtly, the doctor left the room, his heart weary. He was now going to do what he hated most about his job.

He had to tell a grieving family member their loved one was gone forever.

Richard opened his eyes and looked around, seeing nothing.

He was cold, really cold.

It was utterly quiet, not as much as a cough or a footstep to break the silence.

Quite a change of pace to where he was a few seconds ago.

Or so it seemed.

He didn't know how he could have gotten to where he was so fast, but he was here so he might as well deal with it.

Moving his head, he could hear the soft rub of material and he realized there was a sheet over him. Reaching up, he pulled the sheet off his face. It was still dark.

With a choice of lying in the dark or getting up, he chose the latter, so with slow, jerky movements he did just that.

His feet hung off the side of the table, and in the total blackness it felt like if he slid off whatever he was sitting on, he would fall into a black hole. But of course that was ridiculous. If there was a void below him, then how could the table or bed or whatever he was on be there at all?

He slid off the table and his bare feet slapped against the floor.

He stumbled forward, hands out in front of him as he tried to find his way around like a blind man. He bumped into something and it moved with him, so he pushed it out of the way, whatever it was rolling across the floor.

It was so dark he couldn't see his hand in front of his face.

He reached a wall, slapped it, not feeling the cold surface of the metal. In fact, he felt nothing at all. It was like he was in one of those temperature-controlled mediation chambers.

His head was foggy, too, and he couldn't think straight.

He moved about the room some more and bumped into another obstacle. Was this one the same one as before?

He reached out and felt what it was. Though his sense of touch was almost gone, he was just able to detect the curves and softness of what had to be an animal or a body.

A body?

But if that was so, then that could only mean . . .

No, impossible, hospitals didn't make mistakes like that.

Suddenly, there was the sound of a latch being pulled and then bright, white light flooded into the room, temporarily blinding him.

He blinked multiple times before his eyes focused. Turning around, he saw the obstacles were bodies on gurneys, each one with a sheet over the face and torsos and a small tag on each of their left toes.

He glanced down at his own left toe and saw a tag there as well. And he was naked.

None of this made sense. He wasn't dead. He was standing here feeling fine. Sure, he was not at his peak, but who would be after what he'd just been through?

Someone was gonna pay and pay big, he thought. Maybe a big lawsuit or, better yet, a large cash settlement. After all, what hospital would want it getting out they had placed a living patient in the morgue and left him alone, right down to placing a toe tag on his foot?

For the first time he realized he wasn't alone in the room. A man wearing a security guard uniform stood in the doorway.

An armed security guard.

The man shook as he screamed and pointed at Richard. Richard tried to speak, to tell the man he was all right, that this was all a big mistake.

Then Richard watched the security guard do something he would never have believed possible, at least not to him.

The man pulled his gun and aimed it at him.

Richard tried to speak again, but only garbled noises came out. He reached for the man, trying to calm him down, not wanting him to do anything rash. He took a few steps toward the man while still trying to speak.

Hal Stevenson stood at the door to the morgue. His eyes widened, his jaw went slack. The guy they had brought in two hours ago was walking around! And he was buck naked! That was impossible. He had seen the guy with his own eyes when they rolled him into the freezer. Half his face had been bashed in and the body had a massive hole in its abdomen from where a piece of metal had impaled the man when he'd been struck by the cement truck.

Hal knew all about Richard's accident. He loved hearing about the really gory cases in all their glorious details. He was a big horror fan and this was the best he could get for action in his quiet job at the hospital. But what was standing in front of him was way more than he bargained for. Hal had seen enough horror movies, zombie movies in particular, to know one when he saw one. And the naked corpse was doing exactly what a zombie should being doing.

The creature stumbled around, moaning and groaning, then even raised its arms in the air like Frankenstein as it came at him.

Well, Hal wasn't gonna be lunch for a zombie, that was for sure.

So pulling his gun—one he had never fired before—he flicked off the safety and screamed at the creature.

"Stay back, you . . . you thing! I'll shoot, so help me, I'll shoot!"

But the zombie ignored the warning and continued forward.

Hal closed his eyes and fired his revolver three times, each shot striking the zombie in the chest and torso.

When he opened his eyes, he screamed. The zombie hadn't stopped moving and had now reached him. Hal dropped the gun in sheer terror, wet himself and, panicking, tried to run away.

The zombie held him firm.

Richard had felt the bullets strike him and he grunted with each impact, but the odd thing was they didn't hurt.

Glancing down at his chest, he noticed there was no blood either, only three round holes like someone had poked their finger into a mound of clay.

The security guard was yelling at him and Richard found himself growing angry, and then more angry than he could ever remember being.

This man had shot him!

He was a patient and he had just been shot!

He held the guard tighter and . . . something happened to him, something he couldn't explain.

Hunger.

Not just a little peckish, like he could go for a salad, but so hungry it was like he had been lost in the woods for three days and hadn't had eaten a thing.

As he stared at the security guard, he saw the veins pulsing on the man's neck, each pulse equal to the fellow's beating heart, and it was like someone had rung the dinner bell.

What Richard did next happened so fast he couldn't have stopped himself if he'd wanted to. He grabbed the security guard by the arms and leaned into the man's neck, his teeth opening wide as his jaws bit deep.

Blood flowed down his throat and the guard screamed, but Richard's grip was like iron. He chewed like a homeless man eating a free turkey leg on Thanksgiving, tearing hunks of the man's flesh out with each bite. The guard's arms jerked; blood gushed from his wound in pints.

Richard continued feeding. He let the body drop to the floor then knelt down and began gnawing on the guard's right arm.

He did this for more than ten minutes until the guard began to stir again.

Richard didn't know why, but for some reason the instant the guard stirred, the man's flesh became unappetizing. Standing up and backing away, he watched the guard stand on wobbly legs. His head was at a slight angle thanks to all the muscles and flesh Richard had eaten, but the man could function well enough.

Richard was hungry, the feeling of starvation still there. Though he had quelled it for a short span of time while munching on the security guard, the hunger was already coming back worse than before.

Turning to head down the hallway, he walked in plodding steps, not really knowing where he was going.

The security guard followed.

At the end of the hallway was an elevator.

When Richard approached the elevator doors, they cycled open.

Whether it was coincidence or some remaining intelligence from when he was alive, he stepped inside the car. The security guard followed like a lost puppy and when they were both inside the car, the elevator doors closed softly.

For a long time, the two zombies stood in the elevator, not moving, merely staring at the lighted numbers.

But then the car began to move after one of the lights above lit up.

With a soft jolt, the elevator rose silently while the two newborn ghouls waited patiently.

"Come on, Rose, push, you can do it!" the doctor yelled while standing at the foot of the hospital bed in Room 232 on the second floor.

In front of him Rose Rodriquez was in pain, the baby in her body refusing to come out and embrace the world.

"Come on, Rose, I can see the head. It's almost out," the doctor said but in his mind knew if the baby didn't come soon, he would have to consider a C-section. The woman had been dilated for almost a day and he was growing more worried with each passing minute. And to top it off, the woman had refused an epidural, citing she wanted a natural, drug-free birth. He applauded her strength, but if he had been a woman, and in her shoes, he would have been screaming for drugs and as many as they would give him.

"I can't, Doctor, I can't!" Rose screamed, her thick Spanish accent making it almost impossible to make out what she was trying to say. She was all alone in this birth, her husband and family back in Mexico. Her eyes were closed and sweat covered her face in thin streams that dripped down her body, soaking the sheets.

"Yes, you can. You just need the proper motivation," the doctor said.

A naked man covered in blood and a security guard with half his neck gone and a large part of one arm missing stepped into the room, both looking like they'd been through a war together thanks to the amount of gore covering both their bodies.

The doctor stood, staring at the two men. "What are you two doing in here? This woman is having a baby! Get out! Nurse, Nurse—where's the nurse? Someone call security. I mean, *more* security. These guys're obviously sick and wounded."

One of the men raised his arms and moved closer. The doctor brought his hands up to push him away.

"Do you know who I am? I'm the head of pediatrics. This is my floor. Now get out of here before I have you arrested!"

But his threats fell on deaf ears and whatever he thought might happen next, he never expected what *did* happen.

Richard pushed past the man's hands and grabbed the doctor's head, shoving him to the bed right between the woman's open legs. Richard's jaw opened so wide it threatened to unhinge and came down fast. Teeth clamped on flesh. The doctor howled.

The security guard moved in and sunk his teeth into the doc's meaty thigh.

The doctor screamed and pushed Richard away from him, and as he stood up, the blood from his carotid artery shot outward, bathing the woman in warm blood.

She screamed in terror. A baby shot out from between her legs like a baseball fired from an automated pitcher.

The doctor was on the floor and the baby bounced on his stomach. The jolt caused the baby to animate and a high-pitched scream filled the room.

"My baby! Where's my baby!" the woman screamed as she tried to see her child.

But Richard saw it first.

Ignoring the doctor, the security guard now getting the screaming man to himself, Richard reached out and picked up the baby by one tiny leg.

The woman screamed like she was about to die, but first it was her baby's turn.

Richard never slowed, never halted. If he had still been human, he might have given a second thought to eating a newborn baby, but as a zombie, well, meat was meat.

Teeth clamped on small fingers and ripped them off like they were frog's legs. He grabbed both of the small legs, one in each hand, and pulled them apart, ripping the screaming baby in two. The screaming ceased and tiny organs and blood splashed to the floor. Richard ignored them, chewing on the soft flesh like it was veal.

The woman shrieked and tried to get up, but couldn't. Richard noticed the tears filling her eyes. She shook her head back and forth, but he didn't care. Instead he thought of how plump and juicy she looked

His face and torso covered in newborn blood, he turned toward her.

Stepping the three feet to her bedside, he reached out and grabbed her face with his bloodied hands. She was still screaming, her mouth open, her tongue flapping around.

Richard reached in and grabbed her tongue; the woman's screaming abruptly stopped.

With the strength of the dead, Richard yanked her tongue out of her mouth, blood shooting out like a small fountain. While the woman tried to scream in agony and fear, she gagged on the blood. Richard ignored her for a moment, chewing on the tongue like it was a delicacy. The soft, slippery skin slid down his throat like tripe and in his dead brain he realized he liked the tongue, but then was curious for more, so he pushed her down on the bed. While his left hand held her forehead down, the woman's arms thrashing about in agony, he went for her right eyeball. He placed two fingers on either side of the orb and slid them in. When they were in deep, he flicked them upward. The eye popped out like a marble in a hole and he brought it to his mouth. Small threads of flesh and nerves drooped from the bottom of the eye and when Richard had separated it enough from the socket, they snapped.

He popped the orb into his mouth and chewed, a small amount of eye juice slipping out of the corner of his mouth. If he could describe the sensation of that pop when he bit down it would be like eating a whole cherry tomato or a large grape.

Enjoying the taste, he went in for the next eye, but just before he did, three security guards arrived at the doorway, guns drawn.

Behind the men, a charge nurse screamed at the men to just shoot.

Each man fired three rounds into Richard and the dead security guard, but nothing seemed to work. It was Richard who turned first, and as the three men stared at the abomination in front of them, one guard turned and ran.

The two remaining guards fired again and again and Richard's torso swayed with each round. Then he charged the first man and when the man tried to escape, he backed into his partner. Richard grabbed the man by the curly black hair on the top of his head, and yanked back, exposing the neck.

Scarlet teeth flashed in the light of the room and then the guard screamed as a three-inch piece of his jugular was torn free. Blood shot to the ceiling and trickled back to the floor and the guard was dead in seconds. The second guard fired again, three bullets hitting Richard in the arm, leg and one grazing his forehead. Then the first security guard awoke from death and was on his comrade in seconds.

The hospital room was in shambles; blood coated it like someone had entered it with a garden hose and just sprayed red everywhere.

While all this was going on, the hospital staff had just stood in the hallway, transfixed. Easy pickings for later.

By this time the woman was dead, and the doctor was twitching on the floor. Richard fed on the guard he'd grabbed by the hair and his stomach was becoming bloated as he packed more and more meat into it. It was only a matter of time before it simply ruptured.

As the minutes passed, the woman finally awoke and her lone eye began to twitch, flicking back and forth in the remaining socket. Richard smiled at the birth of their sister. With a garbled moan the doctor slowly rose, missing pieces of his face, neck and arms, plus a hunk from his leg.

There were now three security guards in the small room, and as the one Richard held reanimated, he let the man go. The woman slid off the bed and took a moment to pick up a small arm lying on the floor. She began chewing it, the small, fragile bones crunching in her mouth. If she had any qualms about eating her baby she gave no sign. Her missing tongue was forgotten. She had nothing to say anyway.

With the six zombies standing around, hungry, Richard turned and stepped into the hallway.

The staff screamed in panic and a few bolted while others tried to get the nearby patients to safety. With five ghouls behind him, Richard reached out and grabbed a nurse as she ran by him screaming. With her blonde hair in his hand, he twisted his arm and tossed her to the dead doctor. With a gleam in his dead eyes, the doctor immediately dove in and ripped off the nurse's nose with his clean white teeth. She screamed and begged for mercy, but would receive none.

Richard began walking down the hallway on the prowl for more food. The rooms were lined with expectant mothers, and down the hall, after a set of double glass doors, the nursery waited for eager parents to visit their newborn treasures.

It would be a good feast, one any zombie would be proud of.

And best of all, there was enough food for everyone. No one would go hungry today.

When Richard was halfway down the hallway with the once-pregnant woman and the original security guard behind him, the police arrived. Five cops in blue uniforms and weapons drawn charged into the hallway.

They took one look at Richard, the woman and the guard. Then they looked at the three zombies in front of them and the three behind them feeding on hospital staff, and began shooting, cutting into the ghouls like targets at the firing range.

With the zombies taking each shot easily, they soon reached the policemen who tried to fight back.

It didn't take long for the unprepared police officers to become zombie chow and soon enough they joined the ranks of the dead.

Richard was still first and the rest followed him.

In no time, the rest of the floor was being eaten, killed, and then reanimated. After that hour had passed they entered the south stairwell and went upstairs and downstairs, swarming through the hospital and killing everyone they found. Patients who were laid up in bed, some from operations, cancer, or broken legs were all easy targets, trapped in their beds while the ghouls ripped them apart.

Some escaped, but not many.

No one understood what was happening and expected the authorities to arrive and save the day, but none came. The first five police officers probably had never managed to get a call back to dispatch and warn others what was happening.

The hospital, once a place of healing, was now nothing but death, and as the day passed to night in the small rural hospital in the middle of nowhere and everywhere, more and more people joined the ranks of the dead.

With darkness falling across the parking lot and the street lamps flickering on, the first shambling bodies emerged into the crisp, night air. Richard was in the lead, still naked and covered in gore. His upper torso was riddled with bullet holes and his stomach was extended to the point of popping like an overfilled balloon.

Behind him, the once-pregnant woman walked, the doctor beside her. Security guards were behind them and the rest of the hospital staff followed. Patients hobbled out on crutches and some with walkers. The ones with broken legs crawled on the ground, the last in line.

Richard stopped when he reached the front of the hospital, then turned and stood in the middle of the street, swaying back and forth, a rush of serenity suddenly covering him.

Ahead, about a quarter mile away, stood the city, filled with lights from a hundred buildings, looking like the stars had fallen to earth, a blanket of shimmering light that was like a beacon to his dead brain.

Richard took one step forward and then another down the middle of the street, while behind him his army of the undead slowly followed.

The hospital was just the beginning.

Soon the city would know the gentle caress of death and, after that, the entire state, and perhaps in time . . . the world.

The night had just begun and either way it didn't matter.

For you see, the dead have all the time in the world.

SPARK OF LIFE
by
GINA RANALLI

It had begun like it often does—small animals growing increasingly larger as the experiments went on. Guinea pigs to rabbits, to cats and dogs, chimps and finally—lastly—humans.

Her employer, Dr. Nora Fox, considered herself pro-life. With a background in forensic science, she unfortunately had spent much of her life studying the dead—the senselessly murdered, the lost of the Earth. Often John and Jane Does and it was these people that she became most interested in. Who were they? Why had they met their ends in such violent, grisly fashions?

Fox was standing over one of them now—a young woman of about twenty-five. The Jane Doe had been bludgeoned to death, half of her face battered beyond recognition, the skull caved in on the left side.

"Doctor?"

Fox looked up from the cadaver and blinked twice at her. "Yes, Joanne?"

"The syringe is ready."

Mouth curling up in a half-smile, Fox said, "Excellent." She took the syringe and turned back to the Jane Doe. The blue of the eight electrodes stuck to the woman's shaved head seemed especially bright against the marbled alabaster skin.

"I have a good feeling about this one, Joanne," Fox said as she placed the full syringe on the silver tray beside the table. From a box, she pulled out two latex gloves and slipped them on while glancing at the beeping monitor. Eight wires snaked from behind the monitor to the electrodes on the J.D. "A very good feeling indeed."

She didn't reply, turning her attention to a computer on the other side of the cadaver and tapping a few numbers on the keyboard.

"We're finally going to revolutionize the field of law enforcement, Joanne," the doctor continued. "Getting an image of the last things this woman saw before she was killed could potentially take hundreds—maybe thousands—of murderers off the streets. Facial recognition software has grown by leaps and bounds even in the last five years."

Still, Joanne made no response, engrossed in what she was doing. Besides, she'd heard it all before countless times. She'd been working with Dr. Fox for the better part of a decade and though they'd managed to get brain activity out of dozens of corpses—even a few shadowy images on the I.C.D.P—they'd never gotten anything usable in terms of finding anything even remotely identifiable. Just blurs, usually in black and white. Certainly never the face of an UnSub. Joanne wished she could feel as confidant as Fox did but she'd learned long ago not to get her hopes up anymore. Her position and the doctor's experiments had once excited and thrilled her but now . . . now it was just a job, and she was beginning to wonder how long it would last, given that their funding was close to running out. There was only so much patience to go around among the mysterious sponsors of what Doctor Fox called the Image Retrieval Project.

"Ready?" Fox asked, the tip of the needle hovering above the cadaver's iris. Fox held the syringe in one hand and peeled back Jane Doe's eyelid with the other.

A couple more keystrokes and Joanne replied, "Ready, Doctor."

The needle slid into the Doe's pupil, deeper and deeper until the brain had been penetrated.

Fox depressed the plunger; it made a whispered hissing sound.

Once the pale orange fluid had left the syringe, the doctor removed the needle and quickly went about the standard task of taping the eyelid down, holding her hand out to Joanne who already had the medical tape ready.

Tape in hand, Fox looked back down at the J.D. and paused, her brow furrowing. She leaned in closer, studying the punctured eye. Without looking up, she said, "I.C.D.P. reading, please."

Joanne checked the equipment. "Everything's normal, Doctor."

"Curious," Dr. Fox said quietly. "The pupil is dilated."

"Possible reaction to the Arbacell?"

"If it is, I've never seen anything like it." The doctor leaned further over the cadaver and pulled back the corpse's other eyelid, not an easy feat since the damage to the head had swollen the entire left side of the face. Just as she bent forward for a better view, the I.C.D.P. began to beep.

She looked up with surprise.

Joanne spun to face the machine, tapping the keyboard frantically. "Brain activity, Doctor."

Still leaning over the body, Fox asked, "Any images?"

Another tap and Joanne gasped as she stared at the monitor.

"Well?" Dr. Fox demanded, sounding impatient.

Stepping aside in order to give the doctor a clear view of the monitor, Joanne wasn't sure if she was going to throw up or faint. Maybe both.

On the monitor, the picture was the clearest they'd ever gotten off a test subject. Slightly blurry, as though taken by a camera with a thin sheet of cotton over the lens, but still perfectly recognizable, Doctor Fox stared out of the monitor, her image captured as the last thing the Jane Doe had seen.

Both women gaped at the screen for a long moment before slowly turning their attention back to the cadaver.

On the table, the Jane Doe looked up at them with her one good eye and as the two women watched, the milky covering over that eye dissipated, like evaporating fog, revealing a bright crystalline blue.

The eye blinked and Joanne twitched, a small squeak of surprise escaping her throat.

"This is impossible," Dr. Fox whispered. "Impossible."

On the gurney, the corpse's lips quivered, as though it was trying to speak but had forgotten how or why it would want to do such a thing.

Shivering, Joanne stood frozen and did not move when the doctor took a step forward, leaning over the Jane Doe and lifting the eyelid further, carefully peering at the shrinking pupil.

"Why would a small increase of ten CCs cause such a drastic reaction?" the doctor murmured, her surprise abruptly replaced with fascination. "It makes no sense."

Joanne had no answer for her, didn't want to *think* about an answer. Instinctively, she knew something was wrong.

Very wrong.

"Perhaps there was already some unknown chemical lingering in the brain that interacted with—"

Doctor Fox was abruptly cut off when the Jane Doe's hand shot up, grabbing the doctor's wrist and yanking it away from her face.

Fox cried out in alarm, but made no attempt to pull away.

Instantly terrified, Joanne stumbled backward into the computer table. "She's alive!"

"Don't be ridiculous," Fox replied. "We've simply awakened the part of the brain controlling motor skills, no different than if we'd been pumping the cadaver full of electricity. Though, I must admit, to the best of my knowledge this is completely unheard of. What is the I.C.D.P. reading?"

Joanne could not believe the calmness with which the doctor spoke.

The woman *was* a consummate professional, but this . . .

"Joanne!" Dr. Fox barked. "Snap out of it. We need to know exactly what happened here. Now, please, the I.C.D.P. reading."

Still holding Fox's wrist, the Jane Doe used her grip as leverage, simultaneously pulling the doctor off balance and pulling her own body up into a sitting position.

Fox's eyes went wide, her mouth opening into a shocked "O." Joanne finally saw fear in her boss's face. Unfortunately, the doctor's reaction time was too slow as the J.D. opened her mouth wide and sank her teeth into Fox's cheek, ripping out a chuck of flesh the size of a silver dollar.

Both women screamed in unison as blood cascaded down Fox's face. She struggled to get free, attempting to wrench herself away, but the corpse held fast, holding the doctor in place, chewing and swallowing and already moving in for a second bite, this time aiming for the doctor's exposed throat.

The Jane Doe reached up with her free hand and buried it in Fox's hair, pulling the doctor even closer. Even as the side of her throat was being torn from her body, the doctor's pleading, terrified eyes rolled towards Joanne and she managed a single desperate word: "Help."

But Joanne couldn't help. She was rooted to the floor, trembling, feeling her mind snap as though it were a rubber band stretched far beyond its limits.

It wasn't until the corpse released the doctor's body and let it fall lifelessly to the floor that Joanne finally took her eyes off the dead girl's face and let her gaze drift down to Dr. Fox.

So much blood. Spurting. Pooling on the linoleum floor, running like angry little rivers along the edges of the tiles.

Numbly, Joanne was aware she might faint, and she might have if at that moment the Jane Doe hadn't made a low grunting sound that jerked her attention away from the growing crimson puddle.

The corpse swung her legs over the side of the gurney, oblivious to the fact she was tethered to machines by wires. She seemed to want to get up, her good eye now on Joanne, the lower half of her face smeared with Dr. Fox's blood.

Joanne remained transfixed. There was a word for this, wasn't there?

Some silly, monster-movie type nonsense. What was it?

Jane Doe clumsily slid herself off the gurney and stood, weaving drunkenly for a few seconds before starting towards Joanne. She tripped over the doctor's corpse, but somehow managed to maintain her balance, reaching a pasty grayish hand towards Joanne.

It was the sight of that hand waving in the air before her that Joanne's memory banks finally released the word she'd been searching for: zombie.

This thing standing before her, this murdering abomination, was an honest-to-God, flesh-eating zombie.

Joanne almost laughed then.

Almost.

It was the touch of ice-cold fingertips brushing against her chin that prevented it.

She screamed again, stumbling backwards into the equipment, more falling than retreating, and for one horrifying second she thought she was going to hit the floor. But at the last possible instant she grabbed hold of the table, steadied herself and then she was turned around, her back to the approaching corpse, aiming herself haphazardly towards the door.

Behind her, the zombie grunted—to Joanne's ears it sounded like a noise of displeasure and for some insane reason this gave her a spark of hope.

Forty more feet and she'd be at the door, out of there, away from danger.

She covered the distance in what felt like slow motion, her pinned-back hair suddenly falling loose over her forehead, somewhat obscuring her vision. She realized she was still screaming, hadn't stopped screaming since the fingers on her chin and maybe she would never stop.

She might just scream forever.

When at last she reached it, the doorknob felt slick and cool beneath her hand, the door itself blindingly shiny. She caught a glimpse of her own panicked face in the sterling reflection.

But that wasn't all.

Sweet mercy, that wasn't all.

Behind her, there wasn't one shambling, blurred figure, but two.

Breath caught in her throat, Joanne whirled around to see not only the Jane Doe approaching, but Dr. Fox as well, the black, gaping wound in her throat still trickling blood, her lab coat now more red than white.

Clearly dead. Just as dead as the Jane Doe. And yet moving towards her with *purpose*. With *hunger.*

Now both the corpses shuffled towards Joanne, both making guttural sounds, jaws working in anticipation.

Joanne felt the blood in her veins turn to ice water and her legs wobble beneath her.

No! she scolded herself. *Faint now and you'll never wake up.*

With more willpower than she knew she possessed, she turned her back to the creatures and grabbed the doorknob once more.

Only to find it wouldn't turn.

She gripped it in both sweaty hands and yanked with all her might, but it wouldn't budge.

Locked.

Of course it was locked. It was always locked. Dr. Fox never wanted someone walking in on them while they were in the middle of conducting the experiments. Safety first was her motto.

Hand trembling, Joanne reached up and turned the latch, though the sound of the lock opening offered little relief.

Her head was yanked back painfully even as she was pulling open the door, the Jane Doe's fist tangled in her hair, just as it had first tangled in Fox's.

Joanne yelped in pain and instinctively spun around, knocking her own forearm into the zombie's forearm in a defensive gesture. The maneuver worked; the corpse lost its grip on her but not before ripping out a fistful of hair by the roots.

Her yelp became a scream, but her mind would only allow her to feel the pain for a micro-second and she continued to throw herself through the open doorway and into relative safety.

Once in the vacant, sterile hallway, with its ridiculously bright fluorescent lights, she almost felt as though she'd just awoken from a particularly realistic nightmare.

The illusion lasted for only a single tick of time, however, as the zombies in the lab let out a chorus of frustrated grunts.

Debating on whether or not to flee down the hall in search of help, Joanne hesitated there on the other side of the threshold. Was anyone else even in the building at this late hour? She couldn't be sure, but even if there was, she knew she'd just be putting that other person in danger.

She couldn't do that.

Instead, she rushed forward, grasped the doorknob yet again and began pulling the door closed, intending to trap the Jane Doe and the doctor inside the lab.

Before she closed it all the way, she caught a glimpse of the Jane Doe shoving the fistful of hair she'd ripped from her head into her mouth and trying to chew it. The sight was so surreal that Joanne slowed down, completely astonished, her brows knitting together in a flash of puzzlement.

Through the six inches of open doorway, Doctor Fox's ravaged face appeared, grinning wildly, and though she gasped in surprise, Joanne was momentarily relieved to see the doctor smiling. It was a joke after all. Just a joke.

For the second time, Joanne almost laughed and then the doctor reached through the six inches of empty space and grabbed her around the throat with an inhuman strength, squeezing the air from her windpipe, causing her eyes to instantly bulge and water.

Fox shoved her weight forward, propelling Joanne backwards until she collided with the hallway's far wall, her head bouncing off with a dull smack that left her seeing stars and her stomach roiling.

She blinked rapidly, fighting to stay conscious, but immediately wished she *wasn't* conscious after all as the doctor's face filled her vision and became her entire world.

Joanne shrieked as Fox sank her teeth into her nose and thrashed her head like a dog with a rag doll. There was a sound like wet meat tearing followed by the snapping of cartilage. Joanne instantly tasted blood and sank to the floor as the doctor released her, too busy chewing her prize to go for a second bite just yet.

Crumpled, her back against the wall, head lolling to one side, Joanne listened to the rapid drumming of her blood hitting the floor with loud splats. When she tried to bring a hand up to her face, she found that her arm was much too heavy to lift and so she just sat, suddenly craving sleep.

An unknowable amount of time later—probably mere seconds though perhaps minutes—she watched two sets of feet shamble past, smearing the tiny lake of her blood as they went. One pair wore sensible brown shoes and the other—dirty, gray and purple, with yellowed toenails—was completely barefoot.

She felt the growing need to follow the bright red footprints they left in their wake.

IN THE BLOOD
by
ERIC S. BROWN

Detective Gregory stood in the dampness of the morning fog watching the other officers scurrying around the crime scene, making sure it was properly sealed off. He reached into the pocket of his trench coat, produced a cigarette and promptly fired it up.

Becca sat leaning over what was left of victim's body, her long red hair pulled back into a tight ponytail above her forensics uniform. Gregory walked over to where she was collecting samples of the strange black blood that seemed to leak from every orifice of the corpse.

"Morning, Becca," he said, extending a hand to help her to her feet as she finished. She tucked the vials away inside her kit. "What do you make of this mess?"

Becca shook her head. "Beats me. There's no obvious signs of a struggle. No apparent trauma to the body. It looks like this man died from some weird disease and someone just dumped his body here." She slipped off her gloves and disposed of them, then quickly disinfected her hands. "I think we need to call in the C.D.C. on this one as soon as possible. If whatever killed him is contagious, we're all in real trouble and this crime scene has been grossly mishandled."

"So it's not a murder, then?" Gregory asked.

"Does that disappoint you, Detective?"

Gregory laughed. "No. My gut tells me this is a homicide. The first boys on the scene found a used syringe near this spot. I've had it sent to your lab. I'll wager whatever killed this gent was in it."

"I hope you're right," Becca said, looking back at the corpse again. Its features were contorted in a mask of pain and its clothes were drenched in its own putrid blood.

"See you later?" Gregory asked.

"You can count on it," she said, hefting her kit and heading out of the crime scene to her car.

Gregory stood and watched her go. Sometimes she took his breath away.

"John!" a voice called from behind him. Carlson came running up. The portly man was flushed and out of shape. "We got the prints back. No record of anything. He's clean. This guy never even got a speeding ticket. His name was Richard North. Worked as a janitor at a retail store in the city. No family we could find."

"Great," Gregory said sarcastically, scowling.

"Not much to go on until Dr. Abbott sends us her findings from the syringe."

Gregory tossed the butt of his cigarette into the grass. "Keep this area contained just in case I'm wrong about this not being a virus, and call me the second you hear from Becca."

"Where are you going?" Carlson shouted after him as he headed towards his car.

"The store where this poor guy worked. Might as well check it out. Somebody there might know something."

Gregory eased his car into a space in front of the small grocery store. He turned off the Johnny Cash music that blared from the car's speakers and hopped out onto the street still mouthing the lyrics of "The Wanderer" to himself. He looked up at the battered and worn sign above the store. BUB'S. He chuckled. The owner apparently was not exactly a marketing genius. He made his way inside through the glass front door to the sound of the jingling bells that hung tied to its interior handle.

A young, pimply-faced man awaited him behind the counter. Gregory flashed his badge. "You Bub?"

The youth turned pale, shaking his head. "No, sir. Mr. Gallow is out today. Can I help you?" he babbled so fast it sounded like a single sentence.

Gregory instinctively knew the kid was terrified of something. He leaned forward onto the counter, making a point to brush his coat aside enough for the kid to see the top of his .44 where it rested in the holster on his hip. "Look, I need to speak with Mr. Gallow. Do you know how I can reach him?"

"What's this about?" the kid asked, nervous. His name badge read WALTER.

"Walter . . ." Gregory started but was cut off mid sentence as Walter broke down.

"I don't know anything about the porn in the backroom, I swear. I don't sell it. I don't watch it. All that stuff is Mr. Gallow's. He handles it all."

"Walter," Gregory almost yelled, trying to get the kid to shut up. "I'm not here about that. I don't care."

"Mr. Gallow said never to give out his number but it's in the rolodex. Help yourself to it." Walter plopped the spindle of index cards onto the countertop in front of the detective. Gregory pocketed it knowing Walter wouldn't protest. He turned to leave but not before seeing relief flood across Walter's face like water breaking through a dam.

Gregory stepped into the heat of the noon day sun and checked his watch. It was lunch time but there was still a lot to be done. His cell rang, vibrating within the confines of his coat pocket. He pulled it out.

Good, he thought, *Becca's on the ball today.*

Flipping it open, he lifted it to his ear as chaos erupted across the street from where he stood. A man bleeding black fluid came charging from an alleyway. The man looked . . . feral. He hurled himself at the closest person, tackling a man in an expensive business suit. The pair toppled to the concrete with the bleeder on top.

"Call you back!" Gregory barked and pocketed his phone. He sprinted across traffic towards the grisly scene unfolding before him as the pedestrians fled screaming. He yanked his .44 Magnum from the holster under his coat.

"Freeze! Police!" he yelled at the bleeding man.

The man paid him no heed and buried his teeth in the business man's cheek. As Gregory closed to within feet of the bleeder, he leveled his gun at him. The bleeding monster glanced up at the detective with rage and pain-filled eyes. Strains of the business man's flesh dangled from his teeth. With an animal-like roar, the bleeder leapt to his feet, charging at Gregory. The detective's Magnum thundered. The round hit the man dead center in the chest, sending him sprawling backwards to land hard on the street's pavement. Gregory cursed as the man sat up, pulling himself to his feet.

Gregory knew the bleeder should be dead or at least hurting so bad he was nearly immobile. He popped off two more rounds in rapid succession. Again the man fell only to get to his feet again with large gapping holes in his torso. The black blood poured from his wounds at a rate that made Gregory wonder how the man hadn't bled out already. He ignored his own confusion and fear, leaving the questions for later, taking careful aim as the man ran at him howling like a mad dog. His fourth round blew the bleeder's head to a pulp. This time the man went down and stayed there. The corpse lay still in a puddle of black filth. Sirens of beat cops already on their way to the scene filled the air. He holstered his gun and took a moment to catch his breath and collect himself. This case was getting flat out weird.

"So it's not a virus?" he asked Becca as the two of them stood over the corpse of the second bleeder in her lab.

"No, not in the normal sense, at least. If it were, I would have the C.D.C. here on their way whether you wanted them or not. There's . . . something in his blood stream. I know that for sure but as to what it is, your guess is as good as mine. It's like something from a cheap sci-fi film."

"Mind if I take a look?"

"Knock yourself out," Becca said, gesturing to a microscope on one of the nearby tables. "I have a sample set up over there."

Gregory peered into the magnified blood cells. "What are those things? They look like tiny, little robots."

"Nano-bots. Yeah, I know." She seemed to agree with the apparent look of shock on his face. "They appear to be repairing the blood cells but altering them in the process."

"Well, the good news is it's not a virus. This means the thing with the bleeding isn't contagious right?"

"Not entirely," she said. "They seem to be multiplying in the blood sample even though it's dead. If a batch of them crossed to another person through an open wound, in theory, they'd infect that person as well, growing in numbers inside them just like they did in the original host. That black taint to the host's blood that we've seen is actually the nano-bots themselves grown so great in number their color is visible to the naked eye."

"Is it likely they'd spread like that?"

"I don't have a clue what those things really are much less whether or not they'll spread, though I do *think* they could. All I have is theories. Nanotech on this level is supposed to be years away from even testing. I can tell you, though, that a host infected with them will become violent and insane from the amount of pain they'd be experiencing from the nano-bots' tinkering inside them." Becca paused. "You need to get some rest. You were going nonstop before this case landed in your lap. From what I hear, you don't have a single real lead yet."

"I do now," Gregory said. "No rest for the wicked. Besides, whoever made these things needs to be stopped now, not tomorrow."

"You're not a superhero," she said. "There can't be too many places in the city where someone can get the materials to make something like these things, and whoever created them has to have an advanced scientific background. Let me check around. I have some friends at the university. I'll get Carlson on this, too. You, Detective, you go home. That's an order." She smiled.

"Yes, Mom," Gregory shot back, knowing he was defeated.

Gregory staggered into his apartment. Maybe his fatigue was indeed catching up with him. Before the madness of this case started, he'd pulled a double chasing down a scumbag whose wife had found out he was cheating on her. The jerk's answer had been to chop her up into pieces with a meat cleaver and dump her remains down the garbage chute of his building before making a run for it.

The tired detective slipped out of his coat and removed his gun belt; he rolled it around the .44 Magnum still in its holster. He sat the weapon on the kitchen counter and opened the fridge. Mostly white, empty space stared back at him. Grunting with frustration, he looked over what little there was inside—a spoiled carton of milk, a half used loaf of bread, and a pack of cheese slices that looked a greenish-blue inside their plastic wrapping. Nothing appealed to him except the beer anyway. There was plenty of that, tucked in the side of the door. He chuckled to himself and selected a bottle before going for his chair in the connecting living room. He plopped onto it and unscrewed the cap with his shirt. It felt good to be off his feet. Reaching for the remote, he flipped through the channels until he found something he could tolerate. Cartoons weren't usually his thing but he watched Jonah Hex and Batman bring a rampaging alien to justice in the old west.

His eyes slipped closed as he wished the real world was more like the one that superheroes lived in.

The ringing tone of an emergency broadcast bulletin ripped him from his dreams. He sat bolt upright in his chair as he groggily stared at the news footage on the screen. A mass of people, all bleeding black, were running through the streets on the other side of the city, attacking everyone in their path. The reporter covering it seemed terrified and he saw SWAT officers and national guardsmen taking up positions to make a stand against the mob.

"Yes, Detective Gregory," a voice which sounded like a chorus of demons called from behind him. He whirled around to see a man standing in his kitchen. "They are my children." The man's skin was like water and seemed to swim around his bones as black as midnight. The man wore no clothes and was sexless, only his voice—or rather *voices*—identified him as male.

Gregory glanced longingly at his Magnum where it sat on the kitchen counter between him and the man.

The man noticed and waved a finger. "It wouldn't do you any good, Detective. Please, let's try to be civil about this, shall we?"

"Who are you?"

"My name isn't important. You're wondering how I found you, why I'm here. It's simple, Detective Gregory. Of every living soul on this planet, only you know enough to be a threat to me and my children."

"I don't even know what you're talking about," Gregory said, getting up from his chair to face the man.

The man walked through the counter towards him, not around it. The material of the counter seemed to dissolve on contact with the black mass of the man's body.

"The world is a terrible place, Detective. Man kills man. There's rape, lies, more evil than I can name. I'm only making it a better place."

"How?"

The man laughed. "By making it me, of course. I was once a man like yourself, but now, I am so much more. I was trying to create a way to cure cancer using nano-technology but I stumbled upon the meaning of divinity. Yes, a few died before I refined the serum but what are a few deaths in the name of progress?"

"You won't get away with this. Your children out there aren't invulnerable. Someone will stop you."

"Yes, Detective, they might, but you won't."

The man flung himself onto Gregory. They collided with the chair then went to the carpet struggling against each other. Gregory got in a punch to the man's face and his fist sent pieces of the man's body flying into the air. The face reformed itself instantly. A cold, metallic hand grabbed Gregory's neck and forced him to the carpet, holding him there. Another hand pressed on his jaws, opening his mouth. The man's fingers bled blackness into it. Gregory coughed, choking on darkness, then lay still.

The man stood, leaving Gregory's corpse where it lay and moved to the window. He looked out onto the streets below and smiled at the flickering light of burning fires as he listened to a symphony of gunshots and screams.

NO MAN'S LAND
by
JASON V. SHAYER

Lightning tore across the horizon and threatened to sunder the night sky. Heavy clouds were moving in and Rifleman Andrew Middleton hoped that its welcomed rain would wash away the filth that coated his body like a second skin. At the same time though, he dreaded the rain. A heavy downpour could turn the trenches into channels of muddy water that would spread sickness and disease throughout the ranks of Canadian soldiers.

The strong winds that pushed those clouds towards them did little to clear the air of the lingering smell of smoke, human filth and gunpowder.

Andrew peered out onto the battlefield and watched the crows and magpies peck at the blood-soaked earth. His thoughts returned again to the rain and he feared the muddy wasteland the battlefield might become.

"We attack at dawn." The British lieutenant strode with an almost imperceptible limp through the ranks of soldiers that stood along the front-line trench. They turned to look at him as he walked by, but he didn't make eye contact with any of them. He stared straight ahead, unwilling to let them see the trepidation that hid behind his brooding, brown eyes.

The words he had spoken were those that every soldier on the front lines of the Great War feared more than the lime-fouled water, more than the knee-high mud and waste and blood, and more than being awakened during the middle of the night by a rat gnawing at an ankle.

Leaving the trenches in a mad, desperate gambit to charge the enemy line was suicide. Andrew knew the grim odds of survival. The enemy had excellent positions for their machine guns. Even with the support of artillery, which was haphazard at best, getting through No Man's Land under fire defied any reasonable amount of courage.

"I know of a few boys who will be disappointed with those orders," said the soldier next to Andrew. "I helped a corps of engineers set up the gas delivery system yesterday. Over a spot of tea, they couldn't contain their excitement about the prospects of testing their latest deadly concoction of chemicals."

Andrew sighed and simply nodded. He wasn't in the mood for a conversation. His stomach growled, but he knew better than to eat. He hadn't forgotten the bout of food poisoning he endured a few weeks ago that had seen him drop twenty pounds.

No one else spoke through the night. They were trapped in what they believed might be their last thoughts. There was the odd coughing fit here and there. Andrew heard a soldier or two nervously talk to themselves, or perhaps recite a final confession.

Andrew pulled out a well-worn and grimy photograph of his sister. He dragged his filthy thumb across it in an ineffective attempt to clean its surface. He had failed to keep his promise to write regularly to Elizabeth. Early on, he had put pen to paper and sent letters home. As the grim realities of the war settled in, he wrote less and less and eventually stopped. He didn't want to lie to her even though he knew she would see through his awkward attempts to mask the truth.

As his ship set sail for England, Elizabeth had stood on the deck next to his parents. She wore that soft blue floral dress that made her look like summer personified. While his mother was crying inconsolably, Elizabeth kept her emotions at bay, smiling and waving.

As dawn crept closer, the tension became more palpable. Soldiers paced about double- and triple-checking their rifles and bayonets. The spectre of death awaited them, mere footfalls away, and no one wanted to keep that appointment. The rain never came, but the heavy clouds still lingered oppressively overhead.

Andrew closed his eyes and tried to forget where he was. The day he volunteered was a sharp image in his mind. He recalled standing in line with two chums at the recruitment office in downtown Toronto. He had been swept up in the war fervour like everyone else his age, putting aside the teaching career he would have started that fall to fight for his country.

His parents had been so proud they insisted on a studio photo. Andrew had been embarrassed by the photo and how much it cost them. He was now the only one living of the three school chums. It chilled his blood to think that the photo might be used at his funeral.

He knew that sleep was impossible, but he needed to relax. The dread that sat in the bowels of his stomach threatened to devour his soul.

He thought of a warm, late August evening. A mild breeze carried with it the scent of wild flowers overpowering the stench of death. In his mind's eye, he imagined himself standing outside of the enemy trench and watching a glorious sunset painted on the canvas of the horizon.

"Stand at the ready!" The lieutenant's shout awoke him from his reverie. Andrew picked up his rifle and wiped off the mud that clung to its stock. His hands shook terribly and it wasn't from the damp cold. He stretched his long arms to chase the stiffness from his inactive limbs.

Andrew heard and then saw flares launched into the early morning darkness. The flares illuminated the battlefield in a dull, red haze and revealed that the enemy had also decided to strike this morning and had caught them off guard.

The lieutenant spat a litany of curses and dispatched a soldier to report the situation to his superiors. He pulled off his helmet and passed a hand through what was left of his thinning hair. He put his helmet back on and caught Andrew staring at him. He drew his lips tight and nodded. Andrew's eyes returned to the battlefield and watched the surging enemy soldiers scurry towards them.

The lieutenant was a life-time military man who had initially looked down upon Andrew's Canadian battalion. But all that was in the past now; they had proven their worth over and over again and the lieutenant respected them and was proud to serve with them.

Then, a deafening horn sounded in staccato bursts. The soldiers scrambled to find and put on their gas masks. Teams of soldiers moved to the edge of No Man's Land, pulling long metallic pipes which were in turn connected to the snaking pipes that wound through the trenches.

A hellish orchestra of pump engines roared to life and streams of a yellow-green gas spewed from the ends of the pipes. The jets of gas blended into a thick, billowing cloud that rolled over the battlefield. A stiff breeze blew at their backs and urged the cloud of poisonous gas towards the enemy.

The advancing German soldiers had progressed more than halfway through No Man's Land, thrilled as they had yet to face any machinegun fire. Their excitement was quickly replaced by panic as they realized they were trapped between the cloud of gas progressing towards them and the bales of barbed wired that wound serpent-like through the pitted, dead landscape.

Only a handful of soldiers stood their ground. The rest broke formation and fled in every direction away from the gas. Some were caught up in the barbed wire struggling to free themselves, while others tripped into shell holes and on the dead bodies of their compatriots who had fallen in the previous day's battle.

The cloud of gas moved like a hungry beast and swallowed up the enemy soldiers. The gas lingered over the area for a few minutes before it started to dissipate. Slowly, the devastating carnage that was left behind was revealed.

Andrew had witnessed other gas attacks, mostly on the receiving end, but this was different. A gas attack could decimate an advancing force, but it was rarely an effective deterrent. But, this time, it seemed to have been devastating. There were no survivors.

A quiet discomfort settled over the Canadian troops. They were all stunned by the gas's brutal efficiency. A resounding cheer would have normally followed a successful repulsion of the enemy, but now, not a sound was heard. Even the lieutenant, who was prone to barking orders to cover up his anxiety and nervousness, said nothing.

Then one of the German soldiers stirred. His arm flailed about, searching for something. He then pushed himself up onto his knees and unleashed an inhuman wail that Andrew heard as if he was next to him.

Rising to his feet awkwardly, the enemy solider surveyed the landscape and cried out again. Near him, other soldiers started to move and joined him in a hellish cacophony of laments. They fanned out, chaotically probing the landscape.

"Mortars!" shouted the lieutenant as the soldiers were looking his way for direction. Several soldiers jumped into action and split into pre-assigned groups to set up the mortars. After making judgment calls on the distance and conditions, they adjusted the angle and placement of them. In rapid succession the shells were dropped in and then fired out with a dull plop. The shells whistled through the air and rained down upon the enemy.

The shells exploded around the enemy troops, throwing earth, debris and bloody body parts into the air. The soldiers adjusted their mortars and let loose with another volley. In the meantime, the enemy troops seemed to have been attracted by the noise of the soldiers' chatter and were making their way towards them.

The next volley of mortar shells struck with devastating effects. Andrew could no longer bear to look. Instead, he looked down into the trench at the thick, cold mud that threatened to seep over the top of his boots. After a few moments, the shelling had stopped. Andrew took a deep breath and looked over its aftermath.

He expected to hear cries of pain and the wails of the dying, but instead, he heard inhuman moans that grated at his soul. Most of the enemy troops had survived the mortar attacks and were shambling their way through No Man's Land towards the Canadian trenches.

He spotted one soldier in particular, who had lost his helmet and rifle. His left arm had been cleanly severed and yet, he still pushed on. It was a testimonial to his fortitude and dedication.

Andrew didn't relish what had to happen next. It was up to them to open fire and kill any of the advancing survivors that had made it through No Man's Land. He wondered if the positions were reversed, would they be as hesitant to kill as he was? A part of Andrew couldn't help but admire their bravery and courage.

He brought his gun up and took aim at the closest enemy soldier. Andrew held off his fire as he noticed that his target and some of his compatriots near him weren't holding their rifles. The few that did hold their rifles did so awkwardly as if they had never handled one before.

The other soldiers near Andrew didn't hold back, shooting rapidly. While the bullets hit their mark, the enemy recoiled at their impacts, but it didn't slow their progress.

Despite being riddled with bullets and suffering severe bodily trauma, they didn't stop their approach. They didn't move like soldiers; they moved more like sleepwalkers, lumbering forward with arms outstretched.

They were now close enough for Andrew to see their eyes and what he saw terrified him. Their eyes were completely white: a dull, dead white that betrayed no emotion.

The soldiers closest to the oncoming wave of unstoppable enemy combatants started to panic and ducked into the trench and pulled back.

"Stand your ground!" barked the lieutenant. He ran behind the group of soldiers who had left their posts. He pulled out his Webley revolver. "I will shoot any deserters. Stand your ground, cowards!"

The stream of enemy soldiers fell and tumbled into the trench. They fumbled around, slowly getting to their feet, with more soldiers falling in behind them. The scared Canadian soldiers had regrouped and opened fire. The lieutenant joined their volley, firing until his Webley was empty.

The horde of enemy combatants wasn't deterred by the gunfire.

"Bayonets!" yelled the lieutenant, who cautiously took a few steps back from the soldiers that stood between him and the advancing enemy.

The soldier closest to the enemy was a young lad named Terrence who Andrew had spent a couple of evenings with playing cards. Terrence came from a family with a proud military legacy and he was determined to make his mark.

He did his best with his bayonet, but was overwhelmed by the savagery of the seemingly unstoppable soldiers. None of them had their rifles and each of them bore numerous bullet and shrapnel wounds.

Terrence struck out with his bayonet, stabbing like a madman, but it was like stabbing a piece of meat hanging in a butcher shop. The enemy soldiers didn't seem to feel any pain as they were gutted by the bayonet.

The enemy soldier closest to Terrence opened his mouth wide in a hiss and grabbed hold of him. In a split-second, the undead soldier had pulled Terrence in close and started to gnaw at his throat. The other enemy soldier within arm's reach joined in. They pinned him against the side of the trench and started devouring him.

Andrew saw the lieutenant, still gripping his empty Webley, unable to look away from the inhuman carnage. He could see that the lieutenant wanted to act, but he was in shock, overwhelmed by the savageness of these monsters. Andrew was also mesmerized by what had taken place. Terrence was torn apart and they ate his flesh while he drew his last breaths.

A primal survival instinct from deep within the animal part of Andrew's brain finally spurred him into action. The soldier within him wanted to attack these monsters, but the realist within him knew he would probably end up just like Terrence. They needed to figure out how to stop these soldiers. He had to put as much distance between them and himself as he could.

Andrew took a few steps back, carefully watching the dead soldiers as a few of them moved on from Terrence's carcass and overwhelmed the lieutenant. To his credit, the lieutenant stood his ground and went down fighting. They tore into him with merciless speed. They didn't see Andrew and were content for the moment to eat the fallen soldiers.

He turned and ran along the wooden duckboards that lined the muddy floor of the trench. He ran down a communication trench to the support trench then to a bunker. There, he joined the rest of the soldiers who had fled the scene. The bunker was cold and damp and made of pre-fabricated concrete blocks. No one said anything. Everyone seemed to be in shock and was content to hide behind the bunker's defences.

Andrew consulted the trench map pinned up against one of the bunker's beams. This bunker was at the end of the trench system and the only way out was through those monsters.

Then he saw what he hoped would be their salvation. A few days ago, another regiment had joined them after completing a bold raid of a German checkpoint. During that raid, they discovered a new weapon prototype: a flamethrower. No one on their side had used it yet, but Andrew hoped those undead soldiers wouldn't resist its cleansing flames.

He strapped on the harness and bore the weight of the large can of pressurized air, carbon dioxide and oil. He had heard the soldiers discuss its operation and hoped he could figure out how it worked.

The fear of being eaten alive by those monsters drove him on. A few others regained their senses and left the relative safety of the bunker with him.

The trenches were designed in a zig-zag manner to contain the shrapnel from enemy shells and to prevent an enemy, who had breached the front-line trenches, to fire straight along them. Two soldiers walked ahead of him and two behind. They cautiously retraced their steps back to the communication trench and then pushed forward towards the front-line trench.

A lone soldier stood before them. It was the lieutenant. His throat had been torn open and the front of his jacket was seeped in blood. He stumbled towards them with one arm extended and fingers gnarled. His other arm had been gnawed down to the bone, leaving behind no muscle or tendon for movement.

The two soldiers in front of the lieutenant immediately looked at Andrew, evidently unsure of what to do. He motioned to them to move behind him. Andrew was reluctant to unleash the flamethrower against just one of these undead soldiers.

"Shoot him," Andrew said flatly.

While they raised their rifles and aimed, the undead lieutenant still moved towards them, sniffing the air. Andrew imagined he must now consider them fresh meat, which would explain why the other monsters had ceased to devour the lieutenant. At some point during their carnal feast, the lieutenant's body must have finally died and perhaps soured or spoiled the taste of the meat.

The volley of bullets tore holes into the lieutenant's jacket. While the impact of the bullets jerked his torso back, they didn't impede his progress towards them. However, the noise of the rifle fire did attract the attention of his undead brethren.

A motley collection of dead German and Canadian soldiers rounded the corner of the trench eager to sink their teeth into fresh meat. Fortunately, they moved slowly and awkwardly, allowing Andrew and the soldiers to stay away from them long enough for him to set up.

Andrew unleashed the fury of the flamethrower and it belched an arc of burning oil that engulfed the dead soldiers. There were no screams as the flames ravaged their dead flesh. They flailed about helplessly like walking Roman candles.

The intense heat from the inferno threatened to burn the skin off Andrew's face. Some of the trench's sandbags had split open from the heat and poured out their contents.

A thick, black smoke poured from their smouldering bodies. An appalling odour, which was an unpleasant combination of burnt flesh and hair, and the sharp, pungent smell of the flamethrower's oil, hung in the air.

Perspiration streamed down from Andrew's brow and stung his eyes. He wiped his forehead and saw too late that one of the flaming undead had broken away from the rest and grabbed hold of him. The dead man's face was burnt black in places and in others stretched horribly like melted wax.

Andrew panicked. The burning man's jaw snapped at him and his unholy strength held him and pulled him in close. He could smell the burning hairs of his stubbled cheek as the undead soldier gripped his face.

Andrew instinctively dropped the flamethrower's nozzle as he brought up his arm to protect his throat. The arc of fire continued to roar out of the nozzle, but this time it splashed onto the living soldiers that had huddled behind him. The flame showed no mercy and the victims screamed.

Andrew struggled with the still-smouldering undead soldier. The burnt soldier bit deep into his forearm. The pain was a mix of the searing and tearing of the flesh and muscle. Andrew slammed into his opponent, pushing him back against the trench wall. The undead soldier wouldn't release Andrew's forearm from his mouth and continued to gnaw at it.

Andrew stifled a cry and tried to focus beyond the agonizing pain in his forearm. With his other hand, he fumbled around and found the knife at his side. In one remarkably smooth motion, he unsheathed it and drove the knife up under the undead soldier's ear and into his brain.

The soldier immediately ceased any movement and his jaw finally released the terrible hold it had on his arm. Andrew withdrew from him and patted his smouldering jacket sleeve. The wound in his forearm continued to scream, burning, throbbing.

The other undead soldiers had stopped thrashing about as the flames consumed the last of their flesh. The still-living soldiers hadn't been that fortunate. They were screaming and rolling on the ground in agony.

The flamethrower's oil had run out and its nozzle lay there impotently. Andrew took off the flamethrower's harness and dropped its empty can with a hollow thud.

He knew he needed to keep moving to stay alive. There was no telling how many other undead soldiers roamed the trenches. Only one of the soldiers had survived the accident with minor burns and followed him; the others, he begrudgingly left behind.

Then, a shower of shrapnel from an explosive artillery shell rained down on them. They threw themselves against the walls of the trench.

The artillery bombardment was relentless and, as it got closer, the earth began to shake. The continuous stream of roaring explosions made Andrew's ears ring. The bunker was the safest place, but it was also a dead end that would trap them.

He then realized that the bombardment was coming from their side. The Germans didn't have any heavy artillery on their side and proved that when they launched their morning raid.

Somehow word must have reached command about the undead soldiers and their resistance to injury. It was the only logical thing to do: contain the threat by destroying the front lines and hope that nothing could get through.

The carnage they had witnessed in the last few moments proved to be too much for the soldier who followed him. He refused to continue, staring at the trench wall, and let his rifle fall from his hands. Tears cut through the filth that was layered on his cheeks.

Andrew grabbed his arm and pulled, hoping to get him to keep moving. He couldn't budge him. The soldier then slowly turned to look at him. Andrew saw through the young man's eyes that his mind was shattered.

Andrew released him and left the soldier behind. He climbed the side of the trench. The burning pain was gone from the wound in his forearm and was replaced by a strange numbness.

The landscape surrounding the trench system was desolate, ravaged by the bombardments. He looked back over his shoulder at the trenches that now seemed to be wounds cut deep into the Earth itself. He heard the odd rifle shot and saw the grey smoke that rose from the devastation caused by the flamethrower.

He turned his back on the carnage, on his fellow soldiers, on the war, on man's insanity, and ran.

Andrew ran until exhaustion overtook him in a small wooded area. Face down in a bed of leaves, he slept fitfully with nightmares of his dead school chums clawing at him, eating him while he watched helplessly.

He awoke cold and wet and struggled with his heavy limbs to get to his feet. His dead eyes couldn't appreciate the lavish beauty of the sun that was setting on the horizon. The only thing that drove him now was his hunger.

MR. HANSON GOES
TO THE LAB
by
MICHAEL CIESLAK

The steel doors closed with a hiss. Representative George Hanson swallowed hard and looked at the others. Despite the fact that the elevator was a ten-by-ten cube, the five men stood close enough that their shoulders were almost brushing. They followed proper elevator etiquette: Each man stood silently, watching as the numbers descended.

One man stood slightly apart from the others. The five huddled together all wore similar clothing—dark suits, white shirts, subdued ties. The sixth man wore tan chinos. A blue hospital scrub top covered a white T-shirt. A long lab coat completed his attire. Once white, it had faded to a dingy color closer to yellowed ivory. A Rorschach of stains dotted the front and sides.

The elevator hummed to a stop. The number read SL12. The man in the lab coat roused himself with a shake.

"Just a moment, gentlemen," he said as the doors slid open. He thumbed a button and the doors whispered closed again. He removed a key card from the pocket of the scrub top and slid it into a slot on the control panel beneath the buttons. He then leaned forward, staring at a flat black panel.

"To access the lower levels of the facility," he said without turning, "requires two forms of identification. The first is our ID badge."

He held the plastic card up for the men to see.

"The chips are an integral part of the card, making duplication almost impossible. The lift also requires an optical scan."

He tapped the glass square with the card.

"If the eyeball does not match the identity on the card, lockdown. If the card's owner does not have correct clearance, lockdown. There are a number of other security measures in place as well."

He nodded at the men. There was no need for them to know that he had also provided the security system with his thumbprint when he had closed the door. There was no need for the men to know all of their secrets.

"What happens during lockdown?" asked Hanson. He immediately regretted having asked. The other men on the Lazarus Committee had been down to the research facility on a number of occasions. He was the most recent addition to the group. This was his first visit.

Hanson turned to the wall to hide the flush that tinged his cheeks.

"Lockdown is just that: the doors to the lift lock, including the escape door in the ceiling. Then the car is pumped full of a lethal nerve agent."

They rode the rest of the way in silence.

When the doors opened, accompanied by a quiet ping, Hanson had to restrain himself from running into the hallway. He slowly filed out with the other politicians. They stepped into a small vestibule. A large door occupied the opposing wall.

The man in the lab coat stepped around the knot of men. He went straight to a handset affixed to the right wall. He spoke in quick, hushed tones. A light above the door began to flash. There was a loud hiss. The door popped into the vestibule a few inches, then swung open.

Hanson glanced at the door. It seemed comprised of layers of steel. Bolts like one would find in a bank vault were recessed into the three-inch door. At either edge was a rubber gasket that ran all the way around the door.

This level of the facility was airtight. It was far enough underground to be impervious to most forms of attack and nearly impossible to break into.

More importantly, it was almost impossible to break out.

"Gentleman, welcome to zombie central."

A thin, stooped man waited for them on the other side of the door. Unlike his colleague, his lab coat was pristine and buttoned to the neck. It all but glowed under the fluorescent lighting. The knot of a red tie sat in the precise center of the coat's opening.

He smiled at them. The facial gesture twisted his lips upward but never touched his eyes. He ran a hand over what was left of his white hair.

"Congressmen, how good of you to join us this afternoon. For those of you who have not met me, I am Dr. Winston Gilbert. I am the head of the research department."

His voice held the slight tint of an accent. It was not so much a definition of his place of origin as a declaration of his status. Even while smiling and inviting the men further into the facility, he exuded disdain and displeasure.

"I apologize in advance for those of you who have heard this particular 'spiel' before." He emphasized "spiel" as if trying the word on his tongue for the first time. "I tend to be a little repetitive, but I am just so proud of all that we have done here."

He led them down the hallway to a T-junction. They turned right. Behind them, the massive door slid shut with a loud thunk followed by the crash of the bolts sliding home. Hanson glanced back and was surprised to see a tiny alcove just inside the door. Sitting there was a man in a black jumpsuit and matching black cap. In his arms he cradled a very large machine gun.

Hanson and the others had walked past him without even noticing him. The young statesman vowed to be more observant as the tour continued.

The walls changed from eye-wrenching white to the pale bile green found only in government buildings and institutions for the mentally ill. Hanson hurried to catch up.

Dr. Gilbert continued to speak as they walked. "These offices belong to the scientists, who you will see in a moment, who are still working to isolate the specifics of BSV. As you all know, the recent discovery of various strains of Samedi have much of the world's scientific community in an uproar."

The elected officials nodded. Collectively, they comprised the Committee for Research and Prevention of Postmortem Animation. Although this was their official title, few people referred to them as such. Early in the uprising someone had jokingly referred to them as the Lazarus Committee and the name had stuck.

They were the legislative body that made decisions that affected US policy regarding the animated deceased. As such, they were privy to information that was kept hidden from the public. One such tidbit of information was that there were different strains of the virus believed to cause zombification.

"To date we have identified fifteen different strains of the Baron Samedi Virus. Researchers overseas claim to have identified as many as twenty-two, but much of this work is unsubstantiated."

They passed through a set of double doors into an observation room. The tiled floor was replaced by lush carpeting. There were two rows of deep, cushioned theater-style seats. Some of the congressmen sank into them. Others joined Dr. Gilbert at the large Plexiglas window.

Hanson stepped to the waist-high railing. It appeared to be mahogany with brass fittings. The windows were set at an angle, close at floor level, then slanted outward to provide a view of the rooms below. Gilbert flipped a switch and the observation room's lighting dimmed. Those at the window could now see into the area on the other side of the glass.

The area had two dominant features. One was a long table, easily twenty feet from tip to tip. Its metal surface was scratched and dented. Two people stood at the table. Both wore baby blue biohazard containment suits. The table before them was covered with a fine layer of viscera.

Acid rose in the back of Hanson's throat. He turned his gaze to the only other object in the room. Occupying the far wall of was a row of small cages. The cages were stacked five high and extended the length of the room. Hanson attempted to count them, but finally gave up. He estimated that there were one hundred cages. Most of them were occupied.

"Pan paniscus."

Hanson jumped. The voice was very close to his left ear. He had not realized Dr. Gilbert was standing so close.

"Bonobo, or Pygmy Chimpanzee. Sometimes called Gracile Chimpanzee. Possibly our closest ancestors, genetically speaking. Close enough that many feel they, along with Pan troglodytes, the Common Chimp, belong on the human branch of the evolutionary tree."

Hanson turned to look at the doctor. He did so not because he was fascinated by the information, but to avoid staring at the tiny human-like forms in their tiny cages.

"Less than three percent difference between the bonobo and human genomes, yet neither they, nor any of their primate brethren, are susceptible to BSV."

He raised his voice to address his entire audience.

"Nor are any other mammals susceptible. Not pigs, horses, cows nor bears. Not even domesticated animals like dogs and cats that live with people who have contracted the disease. Certainly not reptiles, amphibians, fish, none of these."

He turned and looked at each man in turn.

"None of these, not even our closest ancestor" —his open hand indicated the chimps below— "ever becomes a zombie."

He paused for a moment, letting the weight of the information sink in.

"We are going to find out why."

A few of the men leaned forward in their chairs. This was apparently new information.

"We are currently working on altering the structure of the virus to see if it is possible to infect other animals. At this time we have evidence of BSV being carried by a host creature that shows no signs of the corresponding illness. The virus can be transmitted in this fashion, from human to chimp to another human, yet the chimp never actually contracts the illness. There are no signs of reanimation after the death of the animal."

Hanson looked up sharply. "Is that wise?"

"Pardon?" Gilbert seemed annoyed by the interruption. "Is what wise?"

"You are altering the virus to make it more dangerous?"

"Dangerous how?"

"At the present time, BSV only affects humans. This is a large part of the reason that the initial outbreak was not as devastating as it could have been. We were able to isolate areas, evacuate people before they became infected. Imagine how much quicker the virus would have spread if animals were contagious as well."

A murmur rose among the others in the room. Hanson heard the words "zombie dogs" spoken in low whispers.

The specificity of the virus was one of the few rays of hope that the officials had to offer. Only humans contracted BSV. There were no swarms of reanimated rats, birds, dogs or cows. The virus was a blood-borne pathogen. It could only be spread by direct contact with someone already infected who had died and reanimated. Officials shunned the word "zombie," but it had taken hold in the popular lexicon. The official name of the virus did not help.

The origin of the Baron Samedi Virus, named for the voodoo Loa of death and resurrection, was unknown. Even five years after the uprising there were still no definitive facts. No one could definitively say who had first referred to it as BSV. Since that time, each new strain of the virus discovered was named after some aspect of the vooduon pantheon.

Funny how officials had embraced this categorization system, yet tried to deny what the victims were by providing them with pseudo-scientific names: Postmortem Animates, Fully-functioning Deceased, or derogatory names: shambler, brain-muncher; anything but the word "zombie." A scowl flashed across Dr. Gilbert's face. It was only there for an instant before it was replaced by a smile. That instant was enough to tell Hanson that the good doctor was not used to being questioned about his expertise, certainly not within his facility. The legislator suspected he had just fallen far from Gilbert's good graces.

"The security measures you came through to get here pale in comparison to the safety precautions utilized in the research areas," Dr. Gilbert said, nodding to the scientists in their "space suits."

"Our decontamination procedures are well above code for this sort of thing. There is no chance that the virus is going to make it outside of the facility."

Hanson wondered who regulated the procedures for "this sort of thing" and exactly what other things might fall in that category.

"As mentioned earlier, by determining why our nearest genetic relations are immune to BSV, we will be able to create vaccinations which produce that immunity in humans. The key to that is breaking down the chimp's immunity and modification of the virus." Gilbert was warming to his topic again. "Research into the development of the virus is only one of the many areas we are currently investigating. If you gentleman will follow me."

He crossed to the other end of the room. The congressmen stood and followed. Hanson looked back in the research area one more time. His gaze went past all of the shiny equipment and expensive-looking machinery to the plain wire cages. He thought about the chimps he had seen in the ape habitat at a local zoo. When they weren't scampering around, swinging from artificial tree limb to artificial tree limb, they sat together, grooming and caring for each other. Even at rest, they were alert, animated, in a way these animals were not. They sat; each isolated in its own cage, and stared listlessly at nothing. Some faced the rear wall. Others watched the scientists apathetically. There was no curiosity, no spark.

These chimps might not have been infected with BSV, but life in the cages had already turned them into zombies.

The group filed out of the room. The floor had a gentle downward slope. After a few dozen feet, they were on the level of the research labs. They passed through another armed security door and into a narrow hallway. Heavy metal doors opened off the hall on both sides. Most of the doors were tightly shut. Each door had a slide plate at eye level. Dr. Gilbert stopped in front of one of the doors, slid the plate over, and peered inside.

"It is, of course, necessary to keep a limited number of test subjects on hand. While most of the post-mortem animates are kept in the large holding facility, those who are the subjects of direct testing are kept here in isolation. They can be more closely monitored by the research team and there is no danger of cross-contamination."

He stepped to one side to allow others to view the contents of the room. The first to step up, an elderly statesman from a southern state, glanced through the tiny window. She stepped away. The next, a younger representative from somewhere out east, spent considerably longer. When he finally stepped away his face was ashen. Despite this, he wore a tiny smile.

Hanson was the last in line. By the time he made it to the door, Dr. Gilbert was already leading the group away. He looked quickly into the peephole and started to move away. Then he turned slowly and returned to the window.

The room had two occupants. Both had the gray-green pallor of the undead. One of the animates seemed to have been dead for considerably longer than the other. In places the skin had rotted away completely, revealing bone and exposing viscera. It was strapped to a cot by leather straps across its forehead, chest, waist, and at each ankle and wrist.

The second animate was fresher. In the right light it could have almost passed for one of the living. While Hanson watched, the younger zombie leaned down and bit a chunk out of the stomach of the one that was tied in place. The door was soundproof, but Hanson had no problem imagining the sound of dry flesh ripping. The zombie stood, a stream of blackish fluid drooling from its mouth. It worked its jaws a few times then stopped. It opened its mouth. The piece of flesh it had torn from its cellmate dropped to the ground.

It looked around the room, head tilted. It shuffled a few steps towards the corner. Then it snapped its head around as if seeing the helpless zombie for the first time. It walked back and bent to take another bite.

Hanson closed the door over the viewing window and ran to catch up to the group.

"What is going on in there?" he asked as soon as he was close enough to be heard.

The group stopped as one and turned to look at him. Dr. Gilbert frowned. He arched an eyebrow, then turned and continued walking.

"He just finished explaining that," whispered one of the other congressmen. "They are working on a device that causes the shamblers to try to eat each other."

"Really?"

Up to this point, no one knew why the zombies did not attack each other. Even when they gathered at a "communal food source," new-speak for a human victim, they did little more than push each other aside.

"There are a few problems," the statesman continued in a hushed tone. "The thing sends out some kind of electrical impulse, but the range is only a few feet. Whoever is wielding the thing has to be that close. At that point it is easier to just shoot the things."

"And the other problems?"

"The things only gnaw on each other. They don't go for the brain, like they would with a human. Consequently, they don't actually kill each other. Unless of course, they get lucky and bite through the spine."

"So using the machine would not eliminate the animates, just impair them?" Hanson asked. "Still, it's better than nothing."

"There is also the frequency problem. It causes some kind of brain hemorrhage in the user after only a few minutes."

Hanson nodded. It sounded like promising research, but it was far from being useful.

The group had stopped again. Dr. Gilbert waited for the stragglers to catch up before speaking.

"The worst of the multiple strains of BSV, the one with which we are currently most concerned with is, of course, Bokor."

The group nodded. Everyone had heard of Bokor. The government had tried to keep a lid on it, but the media had gotten word. Panic had resulted.

"Every strain of the Baron Samedi Virus results in the death of the infected. How soon the victims die depends on the strain. Grand Bois is extremely virulent, but the infected can live for weeks after contracting it. Victims contracting the Loco strain hang on for so long that they are often thought to have avoided contracting BSV. On the other end of the spectrum Bacalou and Dinclinsin are very fast acting. Those contracting these strains die within hours. In the case of Dinclinsin, the death is horribly painful.

"The one thing that all of these strains of BSV have in common, other than the ultimate resurrection of the deceased, is that they eventually result in the original death of the infected. It may be hours or weeks, but eventually, the individual is going to die of BSV."

He paused for a moment. His gaze traveled over the group, seeking each man's eyes. Few held his gaze for longer than a few seconds. Hanson refused to back down. He looked into the doctor's pale blue eyes for what seemed like an eternity.

Finally, Gilbert cleared his voice and continued.

"Except for Bokor. The Bokor strain lives in the bloodstream, getting stronger and stronger, but it never kills the host. In this way, it is more like a parasite than a disease. When the victim dies—however the victim dies—the corpse reanimates like any other victim of BSV."

He paused for a moment. The statesmen all wore varying looks of horror or dismay. Gilbert, on the other hand, was rapturous.

"At this point, there is no definitive test to determine whether or not someone has contracted the Bokor virus. None of the various strains of BSV are detectable in the living. It is only upon death that the virus reveals itself. After contact with the post-mortem animated, the question becomes: has the person contracted BSV? If they are still alive after the normal incubation and death period, it is still possible that they have Bokor. Will they turn after death? The only way to know is to have them die.

"Now that the worst of the outbreak is under control, we have turned to looking for ways to predict post-death animation. Lacking detectable physical markers, we have been forced to look for socio-psychological clues. These include specific reactions to certain stimuli."

He pressed a button on the wall and a portion of it slid down to reveal a Plexiglas window. Gilbert rapped the window.

"One-way glass, just like in the televised police dramas," he said. "We have been working on various visual cues. While not every cue is appropriate for every individual, there are certain behaviors that are recognized as indicative of a high probability of post-mortem reanimation.

"These cues are identical across gender, race and age lines."

Hanson turned his attention to the glass. On the other side was a small, brightly lit room. He was appalled to see the sole resident of the room.

A small child, perhaps nine or ten months old, sat in the middle of a small carpet. The baby wore only a diaper. A small patch of thin blonde hair stood up from its head. There was a plastic doll in the baby's hands.

"The test subject seen here is a member of a family which was attacked outside the secure perimeter ten days ago. The other members of the family all succumbed to BSV. Up to this point, the current subject has shown no evidence of infection. No physical evidence, that is." The doctor smiled.

Hanson felt his stomach lurch.

As they watched, the baby raised the doll to its mouth and bit down. It gnawed on the doll's head for a moment then seemed to lose interest. A few seconds later, the baby lurched forward and chomped down on the doll's head again. A stream of spittle connected the doll and the baby's mouth.

"That, gentleman, is a cranial strike. The subject is obviously attempting to eat the brains of the doll."

He pushed another button and a red light came on. A door on the far side of the room opened. Someone dressed in the familiar black combat gear of the Reanimate Termination Squad entered. The sound of the black combat boots caused the baby to turn. It stared up at the soldier, the black flak jacket, black jumpsuit and black helmet. The baby looked up at the gas mask that hid the intruder's face and began to cry.

The wails were thin and pitiful. The small speaker below the window did not transmit the screams of a baby who was scared. They were the cries of an exhausted child.

A black-gloved hand undid the Velcro strap on a leg holster. In one smooth movement, the soldier drew a squarish firearm, chambered a round, and pointed it at the baby's head.

"No!" Hanson yelled as he ran towards the glass. He raised his hand to pound on the window. The baby's cries were cut short, replaced by the deafening boom of the handgun.

He jumped back as blood and brain matter splattered against the glass.

The soldier looked down at was left of the baby. The small corpse twitched once. The head was almost completely gone. The tiny body ended at the neck. The small hand still clutched the doll.

The trooper nudged the body with a boot. A gloved hand sliced the air in front of the armored neck in an unnecessary gesture indicating that the baby was dead. The gun was holstered and the soldier turned and left the room. As the sliding wall obscured the window, the door opened again to admit two of the space-suited scientists.

Hanson spun on the doctor.

"What's the matter with you?"

"Whatever do you mean?" Gilbert asked, seemingly unfazed.

"What do you mean, what do I mean? That was a baby!"

"It was a baby who was most likely carrying the Bokor strain of the Baron Samedi Virus."

"Most likely? You mean you don't even know?"

"How would we know? I told you that the only way to determine infection was after death. The best that we can do with the living is to attempt to determine potential infectees via the exact physical responses which you just witnessed."

"So no one has ever verified whether or not these people have the virus?"

"How would we verify this? Kill them and see if they turn?" Gilbert stared back at Hanson. "Because that is the only way to know for sure. Perhaps you would like us to allow them to live out their natural lives in seclusion. Is that any more humane?"

"Why not just let them live their lives and take care of them *if* they turn?"

"Or we could just let them go about their merry lives, possibly infecting hundreds of thousands of people until one day, through accident or natural cause, they die. Perhaps in a hospital full of helpless patients. Perhaps in an airplane full of passengers. Perhaps in the middle of a church or a school or even a government building. Then, if" —he sneered at Hanson— "pretty big or not, they are infected, then they come back. Then they start attacking. Then they kill and consume and *infect* even more people."

He pointed at Hanson.

"What would you rather have? Death and exponential infection or presumptive measures? Which is better? Wouldn't you rather err on the side of caution?"

"I just don't see . . ." Hanson began. A blur of movement caught his eye. He turned and barely had time to register the black-suited Reanimate Termination Squad personnel standing there. Then lights exploded behind his eyes. His body convulsed and he fell to the floor. He looked at his arm. Two small barbs had embedded themselves there. Wires trailed back to one of the soldiers. Hanson wondered if one of them was the one who murdered the baby. He opened his mouth to ask, but did not get a chance.

Another fifty thousand volts hit him and he lost consciousness.

Hanson's tongue felt too thick for his mouth. He opened his eyes and sat up. The world spun around. He closed them again. Long minutes passed before the nausea abated.

Finally he was able to open his eyes and look around.

He was in a small room. A mirror occupied one wall. The walls were a flat institutional beige. He stood, ignoring the vertigo, and hollered in a raspy voice.

"I am George Hanson. I am a member of the US House of Representatives. You are unlawfully holding a member of Congress!"

Dr. Gilbert's voice sounded tinny over the speaker.

"Actually, Mr. Hanson, our mandate supersedes all other laws of the country. We operate under the same freedoms afforded the Department of Homeland Security, only without any oversight."

Hanson stared at the mirror. He only saw himself. His hair was disheveled. His jacket and tie were gone. His white shirt was rumpled.

He knew that Gilbert was on the other side of the glass.

"Now just sit back and relax, Mr. Hanson. We are going to administer some tests. We will be exposing you to a number of various visual, audio and sensory stimuli."

"Why? Why did you lock me in here?"

"We suspect that you may be carrying the Bokor strain of the Baron Samedi Virus." Gilbert's answer was cool and even.

Hanson's voice rose in alarm. "That is preposterous. What makes you think that I am infected?"

"Well, that is what we are going to attempt to determine. However, I must tell you that many of your recent statements appear to indicate the altered brain functioning which we associate with the infected."

"What statements? What are you talking about?"

"Your willingness to put the lives of the reanimated above the living, for starters. The sympathy that you showed for the reanimates."

"*Potential* reanimates. You don't know if that baby was infected or not."

"Of course, questioning the motives and the official policies of Postmortem Research Facility is a potential sign of infection. As is questioning the policies and motives of its director."

THANKS FOR THE MEMORIES
by
GUSTAVO BONDONI

"I think we're getting something," Claudia said, peering at the monitor. "He's gonna pay his rent after all."

"Do we have an image?" Jack replied.

"Not quite, but we're getting there."

The thing inside the tank had been thawed out a few days before, and it had been a colossal struggle to get it to give even this much information. Now it was just a question of calibrating the image to get some valid data. The hardest part was done.

Dr. Jack Amon sighed, half in satisfaction, half in frustration. *What a way to make a living.* "What kind of information do you think it'll give us?" He refused to think of it as a person: it had been established that all the bodies inside the tanks with the words AMALGAMATED CRYONICS stenciled on the side were beyond recovery—the process that was supposed to conserve them for revival in a better future had killed them immediately. To Jack, they were simply massive memory disks with memories that were messy to retrieve and had to be treated with special care in order not to damage them before their usefulness wore out.

It had cables running out of its nose, its ears and jammed into the base of its neck; it jerked when the tiny electric pulses being used to stimulate its frontal and parietal lobes sometimes missed their mark. The wires led into one side of a computer big enough to interpret the modifications in the pulses and transform these interpretations into images that the biologists had assured him were actually memories stored inside the corpse's brain.

Ugh. "Claudia, what era did you say we might be able to extract from this one?" His teammate was one of the biologists. She had no compunctions about working with dead bodies.

"They froze him in the late twentieth century. Says on his tag that it was in November of 1999. Not a mark on him, and he couldn't have been much older than forty-five. No cancer nodes or anything else I can see. Why would a perfectly healthy adult allow himself to be dipped in liquid nitrogen? Those people must have been sick."

She said the words, but didn't seem to care about the human being that had died because of his ultimately misplaced faith. Her brown eyes held no sympathy at all.

"Maybe he was afraid of the year 2000. Some people back then believed it would be the end of the world."

"How can the possibility of the end of the world be worse than the certainty of dying because someone pours liquid nitrogen all over you and stores you in a very cold tank?"

"That's the kind of question archaeologists hope to answer with these memories," he replied.

"Well, you don't seem to be making much progress." She smiled as she said it, though—it was part of their routine.

"That's because you whiz-kid biologists haven't been able to get me sound in my memories. It's a bit hard to interpret images with no context."

"I'm a doctor. Biologists study frogs in landfills."

"Same thing. Either way, the ball is being dropped on your side."

"Typical of you soft-science types. You blame all your problems on the real scientists."

"Archaeology has been a hard science for some time," he replied automatically. The science here was cutting-edge stuff and the banter was good-natured. No matter what they got from this particular body, everyone working on this project would go down in history, and both knew it. They were just arguing to pass the time while waiting for the computer scientist to return and help them calibrate the image. Experience said that they'd be recording valid visual memories of a century long gone within the next half hour, an exciting thought.

Five minutes later, Oskar Hu returned from his break, clutching a carb bar and grinning at the monitor. "So, the guy cracked?"

"Yup," Claudia replied. "He seems just about ready to spill his guts. All we need now is for you to clear up his eyesight."

Jack sighed. He knew that their blatant disregard for the dignity of death was for his benefit entirely, and refused to rise to the bait. He waited patiently while Oskar keyed in some commands and fiddled with a knob and a couple of cables.

Before long, the image, which had been a fuzzy blue blob, began to clear up. Smaller blobs, not quite distinct enough to be called shapes, but definitely separate from the original overall splatter, began to coalesce.

Soon, recognizable objects appeared—houses, archaic ground vehicles, trees. The technician stepped back from the screen, gave one last tiny twist to the knob and gazed at the image critically. "Nailed it," he said. "Sometimes I even surprise myself with how good I am at this."

Jack and Claudia exchanged glances. He rolled his eyes and she giggled. "Thanks."

"You're welcome. I guess you know the drill from here on out—ideally, we should allow the computer to download all the memories before Archaeology reviews them, to make sure that we get them in case the brain becomes damaged."

"Do you really think I spent all day waiting for these memories to come online just so that I could have the privilege of watching them from a tape tomorrow? You've got to be kidding me," Jack replied.

It was Oskar's turn to roll his eyes. "Why does that not surprise me? You scientists are all alike: you pretend to be serious, contemplative individuals but when crunch time comes you're like little kids on Christmas Eve. Okay, then" —he pointed to the arrow buttons on the keyboard— "forward, backward, still. The numbers on the bottom show the approximate time before death that each memory corresponds to. Have fun. I'll be back to check on you in an hour or so. I've got to power up a little old lady from the twenty-second century."

Jack moved hungrily towards the monitor. While the bodies were being prepped, when power was first applied to each of them, and while the system was being calibrated, he was just an observer. But now, when data about what the late twentieth century had really been like became available—data that had survived the dictatorship's net and library-purges of the past two hundred years—he was the expert. He was the only one who could look at a concrete square and tell the world about the arcane things that went on inside, tell them whether the building was a government lab or an office or a Laundromat. Things that existed only in the minds of certain archaeologists, some dusty old tomes that had survived in time capsules buried for unknown reasons, and, most vividly, in the memories of a few hundred frozen corpses.

"So," Claudia asked him, "what are you going to try?" Her work was done, but he knew she got a rush from watching scenes from the past unfold in front of her. She loved knowing that, despite the best efforts of two centuries of censors from the previous regime, science always found a way to discover the truth. And this was the oldest body they'd been able to activate so far.

"I think I'll wind back to about a year before he was frozen. He was young enough that he would have led an active life, and that might tell us a little about the way people lived back then. We have an idea, of course, but it's like a skeleton—maybe this guy will help us put some of the meat back on the bones." He pressed the back button, keeping his finger on it to speed the rewind process, and marveled at the fact that the highest expression of human technology was operated by buttons, while any household gizmo was, in the worst of cases, voice-activated. The button would never break down and damage the specimen.

He let go, and the image stabilized, the numbers at the bottom indicating he'd gone to four hundred and thirty days before the freezing—a little over a year. Close enough. It stopped just after a sleep period: this was an automatic calibration in the system that allowed them to go through each day in the subject's memory individually.

They joined their subject just as his eyes opened to a darkened room. From here on out, they would be able to see on the monitor in front of them what their subject saw until he went back to sleep. Experience told them they'd soon get used to the subject's blinking.

They watched as the memories took them out of bed and into a shower cubicle. Jack pressed the forward button lightly. Some things hadn't changed all that much. Then they followed his progress with interest as he had breakfast.

"That's bacon," Jack informed her, "from a pig!" He grinned as she shuddered. Score one for him.

But they both winced when he sat in his car. They knew personal automobiles of the twentieth century had contributed to the eco-wars of the twenty-first. But the memories, oblivious of the consequences of their owner's actions, continued, bringing them, eventually, to a squat building of mirrored glass set between a well-manicured lawn and a small copse of trees.

"I'll give you three guesses as to what kind of building that is," Jack said.

Claudia studied it a few moments then said, "I only need one. Set outside like that in a natural grove, it must be a wildlife study station. Or maybe an atmospheric research lab."

Jack chuckled. "It's an office building."

"Government workers used to have offices like that one? It's a paradise." She looked around at their dank underground lab.

Now he laughed openly. "Not a government office. A private company." He could feel excitement mounting. "This is the first time we've gotten the memories of an office worker! For some reason, the people who chose to be frozen were usually more artistic types."

They watched, fascinated, as their first-person view went into a large chamber that contained only a desk, a couple of chairs and an unbelievably archaic computer. They laughed as the user typed in his commands and printed—in hard copy made of actual paper!—five pages full of numbers, which he proceeded to pore over for fifteen minutes after doing so. Then, pausing only long enough to say a couple of words to a woman seated at another desk outside his chamber, he moved to another room.

This room contained a table made of some dark, polished material, which Jack gleefully informed Claudia was wood, surrounded by comfortable-looking chairs. The room was larger than the previous one, and about half the chairs were occupied.

Jack watched in fascination as their host threw the pile of paper onto the table and a heated discussion, accompanied with much silent arm-waving and red faces, ensued.

He turned to her. "Claudia, you absolutely have to find a way to get us sound on these recordings. Do you have any idea the kind of valuable data we're probably missing here?"

"We're working on it. Give us some time."

"Hurry up." This time, his tone held more pleading than banter.

Claudia rubbed her eyes. She was exhausted, but not entirely unhappy. After nearly two weeks of fiddling with the connections and the translation of electric currents back into real memories, they'd finally managed to make sound a viable alternative. And she was glad they had; Jack's good-natured ribbing was gradually becoming more impatient, like a child who quickly bores of a toy and demands the new, improved version. He'd certainly be delighted with this news, and she was weighing the fact he wanted this done as soon as possible against the bugs that still had to be worked out.

They'd realized long before that experimenting on frozen bodies wasn't going to get them anywhere and that they needed a live subject. The techniques for working on living people without damaging them had existed for hundreds of years; it was easy to measure the activity levels when different parts of the brain were actually in use. The big difficulty came in isolating aural memories from visual ones in order to ascertain which part of the brain they had to stimulate to obtain sound memories.

The breakthrough came when someone suggested using the Timing Chimes. Claudia had shuddered just to hear the words spoken, but immediately found herself remembering mealtimes under the old regime. The Timing Chimes had regulated every aspect of life under the junta, and no one over the age of twenty would have forgotten what each and every chime meant. Whether it meant that one should go to dinner, or get up for work or school, or go to bed, no one would forget the Chimes.

So they simply called up the old audio files from the network, hooked one of the lab assistants to the scanner and played the files one after another. Sure enough, a small area on the display lit up with every single Chime. They'd soon figured out a way to plug the leads in in such a way as to be able to obtain the output.

"So," Jack Amon said as he walked into the lab and interrupted her reverie, "have you got my soundtrack yet?"

Uh oh, she thought. She would, ideally, have needed another pair of weeks. But she couldn't lie to Jack. He was paying for all the research, after all. "Yes. We haven't managed to get the memories to synchronize yet, which means you won't get the sound in sync with the images on the first run-through, but you will get sound, and we can line everything up for the deep study."

A surprised look crossed his face. "Wow, that was quick." He grinned. "Great work!" Then he stopped, noticing the look on her face. "Is there a problem?"

"Not really. It's just that I'd like to have a little more time to perfect the process. You see, we found something we weren't expecting and I want to make certain the process we created won't damage the specimens."

"Unexpected? What happened?"

"Nothing serious: the aural memories are based in the medulla oblongata, which we'd never suspected. It's a part of the brain normally used to control things like heart rate and blood pressure—you know, automatic things that keep you alive—so we're getting a lot more twitching and even ruptured some blood vessels. Not pretty, and we've had to tie the specimens down."

"Is there any reason to believe this would interfere with the memory scanning process?"

"Not really, but this is cutting edge research. I'm not certain what might happen if we keep pumping electricity into the medulla. If enough blood vessels pop in the brain during the process, we might not be able to complete the scan."

Jack thought about it for a few moments, eagerness to get his data clearly battling with the natural caution that stemmed from the need to preserve such a precious resource.

"All right," he said. "Have the techs wire all the bodies for sound, but we'll go slowly. You can have one of the ones we've already mined for images to test on. That way, even if something goes wrong, we'll only lose the sound recording, something we don't have right now, anyway."

She nodded, relieved. While she would have waited before inserting the leads into the rest of the corpses, at least this way, they would have something of a safety net.

"We've got them locked in the machine room!" The voice that came over the intercom crackled with static. The leader of the security team seemed calm as he gave the report, but the tension inside the control room would have needed a cleaver to cut through it.

The attack had not come as a surprise—even ten years after the fall of the junta, there were still people who believed that only under strict government supervision could society actually function. They'd sometimes form associations with names like "The Sword of the People" or "The Army of the Common Man" and moved against any organization that went contrary to their way of life. Their scope went from protests and boycotts to violent intervention. A research lab with a stated mission to regain a past the communist dictatorship had spent centuries trying to erase was a natural target.

The security team had been prepared, and while they hadn't been able to completely beat back the unexpectedly large attack force, they managed to keep them out of the more sensitive areas. After police backup arrived, they'd contained the incursion in the machine room.

Claudia, Jack and all the assistants crowded around the vidscreen, which had been partitioned into four feeds. The first showed the police cordon in the corridor outside the concrete wall and steel door of the machine room. The other three showed the interior of the room, in which nearly fifteen men and women, unmasked and unarmored, but armed with repeating sonic rifles, milled about. One of them, obviously the leader, seemed to be giving an impassioned speech.

"I wish we could hear what he was saying," Claudia said.

"Now you know how I feel," Jack replied with a smile. They'd only gotten the first fifty bodies hooked up to the sound system a couple of days before, and progress with the test case was proceeding agonizingly slowly. This attack would only delay things further. He turned to the tech manager, Joaquin Gutierrez. "More importantly, is there anything inside that room that could impair the functioning of our facility?"

"Not permanently. The only piece of important equipment is the generator. We generate our own power because the grid is too unreliable. If they take that down, it might take us an hour or so to get the lights back on, but that should be all. Water will also take a little while to return."

"Good," Jack said. He turned back to Claudia, who was pointing with horror at the vidscreen.

The harangue had ended and the assailants had spread out among the machines in the chamber. They were sticking small slabs of material onto everything that looked remotely mechanical.

"Explosives!" Jack hissed.

"And an EMP bomb. A small one, though," the tech added.

Everything seemed to happen at once. The lights in the control room surged to a high, nearly painful shine that lasted less than a second as the vidscreens turned to static. Then the lights went off completely.

An instant later, they heard a muffled roar and the room shook slightly.

Flashlight beams darted across the walls of the darkened hallway. Oskar was very unhappy to be there, but logic had finally overcome his protests. He was one of the few people in the control room who would be able to tell if the computer systems had been damaged by the power surge after the EMP blast.

He'd argued they should postpone the inspection until the lights were back, but Jack cut off the argument instantly. They couldn't afford to suffer even more damage when the notoriously unreliable power grid was wired in, so if there was any way to buffer the computers, it needed to be done now.

Seeing that that road was a dead end, Oskar tried to convince Jack they should send in the tech manager. After all, the man was responsible for the electric connections. That one fell on even stonier ground. The tech manager was needed to switch over to grid power as soon as possible. Besides, they'd lost contact with the security team when the EMP went off, and the tech team had to find out if they were all right.

All of which left Oskar and two of his engineers walking along a dank, darkened corridor, jumping at every sound, and praying to whatever god they believed in that none of the terrorists had survived to give them a nasty shock. The shadows from their beams danced over every available surface, creating movement where none existed.

It took them only three minutes to reach the nearest extraction room, a small chamber containing nothing but a metal slab for the specimen, a small desk, a chair and the tall shelf that held the computer. Oskar went straight towards the mainframe.

What he found amazed him to the point that at first he thought it was a trick of the lighting, some shadow cast by the flashlight onto the surface of the computer. But he soon realized that while the shadows danced and weaved, these markings stood perfectly still.

"I can't believe it," he whispered.

One of the other techs looked up from the desk. "What's up?"

"Look at this," Oskar said.

The other man moved towards the console and peered where Oskar shone the flashlight. "What the heck?" he said, and then, after thinking about it for a moment, asked, "What kind of pulse bomb did they use? I've never seen this kind of damage before."

Oskar knew the other man was right. Normally, when an EMP bomb was set off, electronic equipment would be useless but visibly undamaged. The console was damaged, however: streaks of soot ran out of the all the orifices and the components visible from outside were fused beyond repair. "Not the bomb at all. The power surge that came afterwards. The pulse must have pushed the generator into overdrive before frying it. And with all our installations unshielded, I'd be surprised if anything survived. These people knew what they were doing."

The second tech, a young woman with short blonde hair, had remained apart from the conversation as she went through some papers on the desk. Oskar had completely forgotten about her and he jumped when she spoke.

"Where's the body?" she said.

"What?"

"According to these records" —she held up a sheaf of hardcopy— "there should be a body in here. On that slab."

Oskar looked where she pointed and saw the slab was empty. He was ready to dismiss it as someone else's problem even after he realized some of the leads that had been plugged into the body were damaged, as if forcefully torn out. But just when he was about to turn back to the destroyed mainframe, he noticed that the leads, before being torn out, had been fused. The surge had gone through them and melted them down.

"Oh no," he turned to the techs. "If that surge went through all the bodies in the storage facility, it will have melted their brains. We'll lose all of them. Jack will have me killed. A decade of research, ruined!"

Gesturing for them to follow, he ran into the corridor, moving as quickly as he could through the treacherous darkness. He was out of shape. The female tech passed him easily and the other guy was only behind because he'd run into some obstacle in the dark. They reached the door of the storage chamber. It was ajar.

The girl ran straight in. Oskar, a couple of seconds behind, saw the illumination from her flashlight suddenly jerk wildly around and heard the beginning of a scream, which cut off in a gurgle. The situation inside must have been worse than he realized.

He turned to enter the room. "What's up? Tell me what . . ." The words died on his lips as, from the darkness beside the doorway, a hand reached out and took hold of his throat. Cold, unnaturally strong fingers curled around his neck, got a good grip, and dug deeply into his skin. Then, a sharp, tearing yank.

Oskar stood in surprise as the flashlight fell to the floor with a clatter and a dance of shadows on the far wall. Warm fluid spilled onto the front of his shirt. He knelt down.

Darkness.

Jack looked up. Frantic knocking came from the door of the control chamber. He moved to open it.

One of Oskar's techs stumbled into the room. In the flickering lamplight, it was hard to tell, but it seemed that his shirt was covered with some dark stain.

"What's wrong?" Claudia asked him. She stood to get a better look.

But the man just turned around, bolted the door, then sat heavily on the chair she'd vacated and put his head in his hands. He sobbed, hyperventilating.

"You need to tell us what's happening," Jack insisted. "We need to know what's going on!"

"Dead," the tech said. "They're dead." A sudden fit of sobbing overcame him and he stopped. He composed himself slightly, tried to continue. "They killed them."

Jack paled, and took the man—more a kid than a man—by the shoulders and shook him. "Look at me. Listen. I need you to focus. Tell us what happened out there."

"I don't know. I saw Oskar fighting with someone, a pale guy. Shaved head. I couldn't see too well, it was dark. They tore Oskar's throat out." He sniffled. "Look at me!" the tech screeched. "I'm covered in blood!" He tore at his shirt, ripping it to shreds.

"Who was it? Was it the terrorists?" Jack was horrified: they were completely unprepared to fight off a terrorist attack. There were no weapons in the control room.

"I don't know. I don't think so. This guy had a shaved head. He was naked."

Suddenly, loud banging came from the door. Another barrage shook the metallic door in its hinges.

The tech screamed and threw himself into the corner farthest from the doorway. Jack just shook his head. Unless the terrorists had more explosives with them, that door would hold.

"Who is it?" he called.

"It's Gutierrez from maintenance. Open up!"

Jack unbolted the door, and the tech behind him screamed again. Gutierrez, pale as a sheet, entered the room, followed by two of the security people. One of them clutched an injured arm and slumped into the chair as soon as he entered. The other bolted the door.

Gutierrez went straight to the circuit breaker box and popped the switches into the on position. The lights in the control room came back on and the monitors gave off a faint azure glow. Gutierrez smirked with satisfaction. "I told Oskar we might need the fuses, but he insisted that while we were connected to his state of the art generator, we'd never have a surge. Hah." He said it in a daze, as if it was a litany to keep from thinking of other things. Then, he turned to Claudia, his face a mask of fury. "It was you. You did this to us!"

"What? Me? Why? What happened out there?"

"Everyone's dead. We ran into . . . things."

"What kind of things?"

"People things. Things that bullets didn't stop, things that attacked the security detail with their bare hands and tore them apart like they were made of paper. Dead things that are alive now. Those kind of things." He glared at her as the shocked realization of what he was implying hit her.

"No," she whispered. "That's impossible."

"Tell it to them!" he spat, and pointed at one of the security monitors where a group of men and women, completely nude, walked haltingly down the corridor.

Jack's stomach did a backflip as he recognized a cadaver that they'd been mining for memories that very morning. "Oh no . . ."

The tech in the corner spoke again, his voice still strained but far from his earlier hysterics. "That camera, what does it show? Where are they?"

As if in answer, the metal door of the control room began to rattle. A solid blow struck it, denting the metal. They all shuffled to the far end of the room.

"Don't worry," Gutierrez told them. "That door will hold against anything short of a cannon shot." He chuckled ruefully. "Funny how you scientist types never seem to want to face the consequences of your actions. If life was fair, I'd send you out there to find a way to stop these things. As it is, you're sitting behind the low-tech armored door I insisted on installing. And that Oskar guy was just as bad . . . and look where it got him. I would be very surprised if even one of his precious computers survived the blowback."

"Oskar's dead, you jerk," the tech said.

"So are a whole bunch of people with a lot less blame in this mess than he had," Gutierrez snapped back.

"So what do you suggest we do?" Jack asked.

"Not much we can do. Just sit tight and wait for someone to come get us out. Pity the EMP took out the phones."

They relaxed as well as they could with the unholy things on the other side banging on the door.

No one spoke.

"Listen," Claudia said two hours later. "Can you hear that?"

"What?"

"The pounding. It's stopped."

She was right. The noise had stopped. It wasn't the first time there had been a pause in the beating, but it had never lasted for ten full minutes before.

"Look," Claudia said, pointing at the monitors. The screen that had been showing the unholy nightmares pounding on the now well-battered door displayed nothing but an empty corridor. "Where'd they go?"

Gutierrez glanced at his watch and grimaced. "Not good," he said. Seeing that the others were awaiting further explanation, he continued. "It's nearly six o'clock. The night shift should be starting to arrive. And they're not locked inside an impenetrable room." He punched the console in front of him, frustrated.

"So they mindlessly go after the nearest human they can get to?" Jack asked.

"Oh, I wouldn't call it mindless. When they came after us before, the first thing they did was attack the cops with guns. Only when they'd taken all the guns away did they come after us."

"Good," Jack said, ignoring the looks he received. "I think I know how to kill them off, then. I've been thinking it over and I have a plan that might work, but only if their minds still function to some degree."

"That's fantastic, but why didn't you tell us earlier?"

"Because the plan called for us to be on the other side of that door. I supposed that if I'd suggested going outside, you'd have lynched me."

Gutierrez chuckled. "Probably," he admitted.

"But now, if we hurry, we might be able to set a trap for these dead people. Tell me, can you patch a recording to the big viewscreen in the cafeteria?"

"I already told you, *my* equipment's running fine! Oskar was the one who got all his stuff fried."

"Here, then." Jack handed the other man a media drive. "Find the file named 'Johnson 1999' and run the images from the fourth flag."

Gutierrez looked doubtful, but nodded.

"Thanks," Jack said. "Now, does anyone know where we keep the fuel for the generator?"

The tech in the corner raised his hand timidly. Jack groaned. "Anyone else? I need to go outside, kid. I just don't think you're up to it."

The kid swallowed but when he replied, his voice was strong. "I can do it. And besides, only Oskar's people know where he kept the supplies for the generator."

Jack looked over to Gutierrez, who gave him a sour look and shrugged. "He said that the thing was designed to last for decades without maintenance. He also explained that 'without maintenance' specifically referred to the fact I wasn't supposed to poke my nose into it."

"Okay. It seems you're it, then. What's your name, anyway?"

"Augustus," the tech said.

"You're kidding. Oh, well, it'll have to do. Come on, let's see if we can get this door open."

Jack'd been spotted. The lumbering, ponderous footsteps behind him were a clear sign the once-frozen corpses were intent on catching him. He'd been appalled at the way they looked: pale white skin spattered with human blood. Unthinking expressions, unseeing eyes.

But the eyes did see. They'd seen him as soon as he'd seen them.

Nothing that had been dead as long as these people should have been able to move that quickly. As he sprinted back, he reflected he couldn't really blame them for having killed everyone they'd come into contact with since being revived; he wondered how he would have felt if he'd been reanimated after centuries on ice. So he ran faster than he'd planned back towards the cafeteria, where he'd left Augustus preparing their little surprise. He hoped the tech would be able to finish before he barged in with a few dozen dead people running after him. He was also hoping the whole group had followed as opposed to just some of them. It would be very difficult to set another trap once this one was used up.

On reaching the door to the cafeteria, Jack didn't stop. He only paused slightly to make certain the man-height screen was showing the images he'd asked Gutierrez to display, and splashed through the two-hundred-foot–long chamber. Only when he was well out of the liquid did he break off his run to look behind him.

The dead were just beginning to enter the cafeteria, moving more cautiously now, as if they suspected something was amiss. Seeing nothing out of the ordinary, they began to charge towards where Jack was standing, praying that his idea would work.

About halfway across the chamber, the charge faltered. It was a small thing at first; one of the pursuers happened to catch a glimpse of the screen and slowed for a closer look. As more and more of the unholy things turned to see what was happening, the charge lost most of its momentum. Soon, all of the creatures were watching, completely mesmerized.

"Now!" Jack yelled.

Augustus emerged from the shadows on one side of the room, quickly lit a match and carefully threw it onto the edge of the liquid pooled over most of the floor of the cafeteria. The liquid—generator fuel—ignited immediately.

Jack tensed, ready to run. He thought the crowd, realizing it was being cooked alive, would immediately turn on its tormentors.

But the undead horde stayed right where it was, even as the flames consumed their lower extremities. They seemed to be in no pain.

They're already dead, Jack thought. *What could possibly hurt them?*

Augustus walked cautiously around the blazing pool, coming to a halt right beside him. He shook his head in wonder. "It worked. I thought you were crazy, but it worked. What are they watching? What are those things with the children?"

Jack smiled. "That's how the world used to look before the dictatorship. They're watching a recording taken from the memory of one of the bodies. I flagged it because I believed it was a happy memory. The green stuff is a form of vegetation known as grass, and I believe the large expanse was once called a park. The things with the children are called dogs."

"Dogs?"

"Yes, we believe they used to be kept as companions for families a few centuries ago. Some records show they were all eaten in the economic disaster after the change of government."

"Dogs," Augustus mused, his face illuminated by the flickering light of burning flesh.

In the center of the room, one of the things, still staring at the screen in rapt bliss, fell to the floor as a charred leg collapsed. It shifted slightly so that its eyes faced the screen, and continued to burn in silence.

HOMELESS ZOMBIES
by
VINCENT L. SCARSELLA

I saw Joe Reed sitting in a booth in the back of Harvey's Bar & Grill, sipping a beer, minding his business. Problem was—Joe was dead. Killed by a heart attack six months ago. He was only forty-five, my age. I attended his funeral.

After squinting back there for a minute or so, I shrugged it off. I waved the bartender over for another beer and tried watching a ball game on the small color TV on a shelf above the bar. But every now and then, I couldn't resist glancing over my shoulder at the Joe Reed look-a-like.

Finally, it was time to take a leak. The men's room was in the back of Harvey's off a small hallway just past the booth occupied by the Joe Reed look-a-like. As I strolled by, I gave him a crosswise glance.

While pissing into an old urinal in the narrow john, I marveled how much the guy truly resembled Joe. The same Joe whose corpse I had seen only six months ago in a brass coffin at O'Connell's Funeral Parlor, lifeless as a department store mannequin. On the return trip from the john, I couldn't help myself: I stopped at the booth and gave the guy a long, hard look.

"Joe?" I mumbled. "Joe Reed?"

He turned to me with a blank stare. Joe and I had once been best friends. But after high school, we had gone our separate ways. By the time we each got married and settled down into family life and lousy jobs, our friendship was a cold memory, nothing more than a couple of faded photographs of grinning, swaggering teens in a worn out photo album. The day I learned of his death, I hadn't seen him in over five years.

"Joe?" I said and laughed.

But the guy didn't move. He just blinked.

"It's me," I said. "Don Kaminski."

When nothing came except a cold stare, I straightened and stood for a moment at his booth. I tried explaining to the guy as coherently as I could without slurring too much why I was bothering him—that he looked just like a friend of mine who had died a few months back. But the nameless guy just sat there, staring forward with those blank eyes.

"Well, screw you," I said and walked away from him.

Joe Reed was dead. Six feet under. I had seen his casket at the grave. I even cried when the priest uttered those last somber words, "Ashes to ashes, dust to dust." I ate bacon and eggs and sipped orange juice and coffee at his funeral breakfast in the back room of O'Leary's Restaurant. Then, I downed several shots of bourbon with his brothers, Tom and Bill, long into the afternoon after everyone else had gone home.

I returned to my barstool. After gulping down the rest of my beer, I called the bartender over.

"You know that guy?" I asked, gesturing behind me with a thumb.

"What guy?"

"The guy back there," I said. "In the last booth before the john."

The bartender squinted that way. "What f'n guy?" he asked.

I swung around.

The booth with the Joe Reed look-a-like was empty.

"A ghost," Betty said. "What you saw was Joe Reed's ghost."

She smiled, tucking me under the covers, glad that I had not stayed out all night and spent half my paycheck in some gin mill. Betty had become a plump and lonesome housebound woman as she approached her forty-sixth birthday. In high school, she had been a beauty. Blonde and tart. Once, back then, she had dated Joe Reed. She said he had hands as swift as water and as rough as sand, and that she was not that kind of girl. She'd dumped him flat and started dating me not long after. But she had cried real tears at his wake and it made me wonder if she regretted not putting up with his swift hands and that crooked, daring smile all the other girls seemed to blush over.

"No," I insisted. "I saw him."

I must have sounded like the complete drunk I had become.

"Joe Reed" I slurred.

Betty patted my head and smiled knowingly.

"Optical illusion," she suggested as she rose up and headed out of the room. (We hadn't slept together in years.) As she turned out the light, she added, "Sweet dreams."

I fell into a deep, dark sleep. No dreams. I didn't wake up until about ten the next morning. The smell of coffee and bacon wafted up from the kitchen. I heard Betty humming to herself.

I stumbled downstairs, the hangover not all that bad. Betty smiled as I fell into my chair at the kitchen table.

"You okay?" she asked. "Hungry?"

"Starved," I said.

I slurped up the eggs, over easy, with a slice of toast lathered with too much butter, and the bacon she placed in front of me. I gulped it all down with a strong cup of coffee.

Betty sat down across from me with her own cup just as I was soaking up the last of the eggs. "Still think you saw Joe Reed?"

I looked up, explaining what I had seen, how closely the guy resembled Joe, even his voice.

"I dunno," I said with a shrug, thinking maybe it was just the booze after all.

"What where you doing all the way out there, anyway?" Betty asked with a doubtful look. "In the old neighborhood? At Harvey's of all places?"

I shrugged and slurped more coffee. I hadn't been to that old joint in maybe ten years. We used to live in a dump around the corner before I got the job at Ford and we moved out to the suburbs.

Actually, I had gotten depressed after a couple of drinks at Dixie's, my usual stop after my three-to-eleven shift with some of the guys from Ford. I craved the old days, old faces. Somehow, I had ended up at Harvey's staring into the face of a dead man.

"I dunno," I said. "Missed the place, I guess."

"But as for seeing Joe Reed there . . ." Betty said with a wave of her hand. Then she was staring off out the kitchen window, thinking of something. Joe Reed, perhaps.

That night, a Saturday, I told Betty I was going to the store for another six pack. I went back to Harvey's instead. And there he was, Joe Reed, sitting at the back of the place in the same corner booth as the night before.

After gulping down a shot of whiskey, I hopped off the barstool and strode up to him.

"Mind if I sit down?"

He regarded me without a hint of recognition. His eyes had that cold, empty look, same as yesterday. It was as if he was only half-awake.

I sat down anyway.

"You're Joe Reed, aren't you?" I was sure of myself, persuaded.

But he remained noncommittal. Didn't even shrug, just sat there circling the lip of his glass of beer with his right index finger, around and around. It was something the real Joe used to do. I shuddered with the sudden recollection.

Finally, our eyes met. That gave me a fright. They were certainly Joe Reed's eyes, blue and wide, but full of loss, not bright and confident as I remembered them.

He swallowed the rest of his beer and abruptly slid out of the booth. Without a word, he started toward the front of the bar.

A moment later, I followed him.

He was a shadow walking down Maple Avenue when I first caught sight of him. It had rained earlier, and the wet pavement and dark puddles glistened in the cold glare of the street lamps.

Staying a safe distance behind and out of sight, I tried to remember the way Joe Reed had walked. This certainly wasn't it. He walked deliberately now, programmed, stiff, as driven by something outside his control.

I stayed with him as he meandered down a series of narrow side streets. Old, grungy clapboard houses hulked so close together in the shadows of this old neighborhood you could almost reach between them. At last, he rounded a corner onto Colton Avenue. I knew the area from the old days when Betty and I had rented a flat in one of the clapboard monstrosities the next street over.

Joe abruptly stopped in front of one of the old houses—111 Colton— turned sharply to the left, and started up a narrow walkway. Crouching behind a tree across the street, I watched as he stepped onto the porch, opened the front door and went inside.

Something warned me against following him into the place. But, of course, I had to do it. I knew I wouldn't sleep again if I didn't find out how Joe Reed had come back to life.

I started down the dark, narrow pathway, tip-toed up the front steps onto the porch and stopped a moment at the front door. Finally, I turned the knob and was completely surprised when the door creaked opened.

Homeless Zombies

Despite a torrent of misgivings, I entered an old, musty foyer. The immediate smell of decay instantly drove me back. It was as if I had opened a tomb and had inhaled the dust of dead men. I hesitated a long moment, struck by the silence and foreboding of this place. But I fought off the dread, stood my ground.

Instead of retreating, I heard myself shout: "Hello!" My call reverberated off the high ceilings of the foyer and long-abandoned inner rooms. I crouched tensely, waiting.

After another few moments, I again called out: "Hello!" Then, I added, "Anybody home?"

Nothing. Not a peep.

Frowning, I pressed deeper into the place, driven by my aching curiosity. I had seen a dead man. His body, at least, had risen, whole and fresh, and walked among us, the living. I had to know how such a thing was possible.

I quickly found a large expanse of darkness, a living room of sorts, furnished with a couple lumpy chairs and a wide sofa with tables in between. I took a step into the room but stopped after a moment, sensing something lurking in the shadows. I leaned forward and squinted, listening. After a moment, I backed off and suppressed a gasp. I knew at once that there were things in that room.

Beings.

After a fretful sigh, my eyes focused upon them—shadows, shapes, a dozen perhaps, men, women. Some were standing back against the walls; others occupied the chairs and sofa; a few more sat cross-legged on the dank carpet. Doing nothing.

As I stepped completely into the room, there were glances my way, but none of the beings approached me. My sudden presence had been acknowledged, but that was all. Within moments, the beings returned to their silent brooding.

Then a soft voice behind me, at the threshold of the doorway I had just entered, said: "They're zombies."

I jumped. My heart pounded. I whirled around and saw a rather unimposing, plump little man.

"Homeless zombies," he added.

He introduced himself as Dr. Heinrich Hulbert; "Henry" for short. He reached out and offered a chubby, clammy handshake.

After letting go of his hand, I asked, "Zombies? How's that?"

"The creatures before you," he said, gesturing to the assembly of listless folk occupying the living room. "Zombies. Mindless, homeless zombies." He gazed at them with a wan expression. "Resurrected from death."

At last, he turned to me.

"You see," he went on, "I have let them go. Helped them escape. Brought them here."

I thought he must be mad and cursed myself again for coming here. I could be sitting in a warm bar, washing down another shot with another beer.

I gave the little impish man half a smile and half a sneer.

"What are you talking about, Mister?" I pointed to the roomful of beings. "Who are these people? Mental patients?" Then I remembered that Joe Reed had walked in here.

"I told you," he said. "Zombies. Resurrected from death. We stole their bodies from the freshest graves, dozens of them. Then we used the most advanced procedures of regenerative medicine to repair dead, damaged tissue and reanimated them, brought them back to life with a zap of electricity. And presto!" He snapped his fingers and laughed like a wizard in a magic shop. "To our astonishment, it worked! They woke up."

Suddenly, he frowned.

"But what woke up is what you see before you: mindless automatons, oblivious to their condition. Without a shred of memory or initiative.

"You see" —and now he smiled sardonically— "each of them has awakened physically, but without a soul."

His wide eyes formed into a deep scowl as he gazed upon the alleged zombies.

"Because of this," he went on, more to himself than to me, "the army knew that the experiment had failed. What good would it be to resurrect a soldier but not his soul? So the project was aborted. We were sent back to the drawing board, to find a way not only to resurrect bodies, but souls as well—the essence of what the person was, had been."

Dr. Hulbert sighed as he turned to the twenty or so subdued beings before us in the living room of the old, dark drafty house.

"As for these poor creatures," he said, "the army ordered them destroyed. 'De-animated,' was the word they used. We had to kill them and secretly put them back into their graves"

He looked to me again, his eyes full of distress.

"That was something I simply could not let them do," he said. "First of all, I disagreed with the assessment they were completely soul-less. I thought I could detect a hint of something, some mental recognition of individual identity, however dim. So I helped them escape and brought them here to this old abandoned house, one of many owned in this city by my cousin, Max, that I was able to rent on the cheap. I hoped that when these zombies mixed into the general population, their souls might be reborn."

I nodded, trying to understand what he was telling me.

"So," I said, suddenly thinking of Joe Reed, my friend. Now resurrected. Now soul-less. "Do you think that can be done? For souls to be reborn? For them to remember who they'd been?"

"We tried to do that, to retrain them, of course," said the doctor. He leaned against the doorway and slid down it in a sullen lump to the carpet. "We tried everything."

He looked up at me. "Perhaps," he said, "we failed because there is no way to resurrect a soul."

"So now what?" I asked after a time.

"Back to the drawing board, I guess," Dr. Hurlburt said with a shrug.

"No," I said, and nodded to the dark room where the dozen or so homeless zombies dawdled. "What about them?"

His eyes flashed up at me.

"They can live here," he said, then added, "roam the streets like the thousands of other mindless, homeless waifs and mental cases that populate this city, ignored by the masses. For as long as they want."

I wondered why he had told me this, revealed his secret. He seemed more than a little nuts himself, stressed out, and perhaps just needing a friend, someone, anyone with whom he could confide and receive compassion. That someone that dark night happened to be me.

Every night the following week, I snuck out after Betty went to bed and headed for the house in our old neighborhood where the homeless zombies lived. I said nothing to Betty about it. She already thought I was drinking too much and probably couldn't take much more of my nonsense before she left me altogether and went to live with her sister in Phoenix.

Naturally, during those nightly visits, I sought out Joe Reed. Sometimes, he wasn't there, having himself snuck out to Harvey's to wet his whistle with his favorite brew. Dr. Hurlburt, I had learned, was well off and gave each of the twenty or so homeless zombies a small allowance for their nightly wanderings. Some of them, the dimmest ones, remained in the house, satisfied to sit in silence and darkness, while others, like Joe, were impelled to seek out the world their death had left behind.

"Doesn't that imply something?" I asked Dr. Hurlburt one evening. "That they are aware, at least of something?"

The doctor merely scowled and shrugged.

"That they have a little piece of their souls in them?" I said. "Take Joe, for instance. There must be a little piece of him that remembers Harvey's, the taste of his favorite brew."

Dr. Hurlburt grinned. "Perhaps," he said, nodding. "Perhaps."

I also set about trying to help Joe Reed find his soul.

The first thing I did was visit his older sister, Mary. At first, she didn't recognize me. But after a few minutes she was laughing over the memories of being tormented by Joe and me with toads and earthworms in the old house where they had grown up.

"You two were holy terrors," she remembered, laughing. "Little devils!" I told her that I had stopped by because the old gang was planning a reunion and we wanted to get some photos of Joe for a scrapbook that could be fondly passed around.

She brought out a shoe box of old pictures and leafed through them while we sat at her kitchen table. It didn't take her long to pull out a dozen or so pictures of Joe in various phases of his life. In one, he was a silly, grinning nine-year-old. There were a couple poses in his serious teenage years (one of which had me in my serious teenage years with our arms around each other's shoulders in a defiant stance). Another was from his wedding day; and, later, with his two daughters, Sandra and Kim, and wife, Judy, before the divorce. "Whore," Mary muttered as she tossed that picture aside. There was, finally, the one from the last week of his life, in which, I had to agree with Mary, he did look tired and forlorn.

"Too much work," Mary said as she gazed at this picture. "Too much worry."

The last photographs she pulled from the box, almost as an afterthought, surprised me: it was of Joe and a slim girl with long, silky blonde hair, standing in front of his father's car. She was staring at him with unmistakable adoration.

It was my Betty, of course, before her first and only date with Joe Reed.

Homeless Zombies

Joe didn't give any of the photographs a second look as I shoved them one-by-one under his heavy gaze in the back booth of Harvey's that night.

"Hey, Joe," I said, finally showing him the one from our teenage years, "look at these dudes. Two worthless punks." I shook my head, marveling at our arrogance, our youth and our disdain for the world.

But Joe Reed didn't flinch. His eyes held that same tedium.

"You're wasting your time," Dr. Hurlburt said. I had invited him to the bar, to see for himself what effect the photographs might have. "You don't think we tried this in our therapies?"

I shrugged as I pulled the photograph from under Joe Reed's eyes.

On the way back to the zombie house with Joe in tow, Dr. Hurlburt seemed to soften a little and thanked me for my efforts to revive his soul.

In front of the place, he turned and looked up into the dark windows.

"Maybe the army is right," he said, "in wanting to destroy them."

I shuddered. In that moment, with Joe standing dumbly next to us, I almost agreed.

But in the next instant, Joe turned to me.

"Don Kaminski," he said, squinting. "Right?"

I looked at Dr. Hurlburt. His eyes were as wide and smiling as mine.

I worked three to eleven the next day and rather than going out with my crew for a round of drinks at Dixie's afterwards, I headed straight for the zombie house.

But the place was a burning, roaring blaze. There were fire trucks and ambulances and police cars blocking Colton Avenue. Firemen and cops rushed around and everyone in the neighborhood was out gawking at the tragedy. I heard somebody tell a neighbor it must have been a crack house. Weird strangers coming and going. And the place always dark, sinister.

I ran past the barricades in the middle of the street toward the house until one of the cops stopped me.

"Hey, bud!" He was a tall, burly guy with arms as wide as branches. "Where you think you're going?"

"I knew a guy in there," I said.

"Sorry, bud," said the cop with a sympathetic nod, "but if he was in there, he's just a pile of ash now." I backed off and gave the house a last glance. It smoldered and stank of old burnt wood, flesh perhaps. Tomorrow, the city would come and tear it down.

I turned and trotted the four blocks to Harvey's.

And there he was, Joe Reed, sitting in his favorite booth in the back of the place, sipping a beer. I hurried over and slid in across from him.

"Hey, Joe," I said, huffing from the run. "You there for the fire? What happened to that doctor guy? Hurlburt?"

He frowned and took a sip of beer.

"Hey, Joe," I said. "Remember me? It's Don. Don Kaminski."

A hint of recognition filled his eyes, then a frown.

"Yeah," he said. "Don."

"Yeah. Don," I gushed. "So, what happened? How'd the house burn down?"

"Bad men came," he said. "Men from the camp. I was coming here. Didn't see me."

I guessed a platoon from the army had tracked the zombies down to Hurlburt's cousin's house and burnt the place down, thinking all of them were inside. But Joe must have been on his way to Harvey's when they raided the place.

"Idiots," I mumbled. Joe expressed no opinion. He just took another sip of beer and waited. For what, I didn't think he even knew.

"You'll gonna have to come with me," I told him with some urgency in my voice.

He looked at me, but didn't seem to care. He was content, didn't have a worry in the world, and in that moment, I envied him.

I let him finish his beer, then stood and said, "C'mon." I reached under his arm and he let me lift him out of the booth.

Betty's eyes boggled when I walked into the kitchen with Joe Reed in tow. She dropped the dish she had been drying in the sink. It shattered. She wobbled away from the sink and plopped heavily onto a chair at the kitchen table.

It took her some time to get over the shock of seeing a dead man.

I explained everything to her, where I had been every night the last two weeks. And, finally, what just happened to the zombies and Joe Reed's good fortune at having been on his way to Harvey's when the army troops came.

"And here I thought you had a girlfriend," Betty said with a laugh.

"Joe needs a place to stay a while," I told her.

Betty looked at him and nodded agreeably. And for a moment, I thought I saw something of the old desire in her eyes. I thought it looked something like the way she was looking at him in that old photograph Joe's sister, Mary, had given me of their first and only date. But a moment later, I shook my head and thought I must be going crazy. I wondered if Betty had any more desire for anything in her life.

"Sure," she said and looked back at me. "For a little while. We got the room."

We put Joe Reed up in one of bedrooms that was for the kid we never had when we bought the house twenty years ago. Somehow, after a couple of days, we got used to having him around.

I went back to work at Ford, and Betty went back to being housebound. Still, it bothered me the two of them were home alone all day. During my shift, I started imagining them making love in his bedroom. All over the house, for that matter. That would certainly go a long way to waking up his soul.

Three or four days after Joe Reed had moved in with us, I confessed my concerns to Betty. She blushed momentarily, and waved a hand at me.

"Don't be silly," she said. "All he does all day long is sit in the living room, drink beer and watch TV." She laughed. "Just like you when you come home."

But I didn't buy it. There seemed something different about Joe after only three days. He seemed more alert, playing at being dumb instead of being dumb.

My fears were confirmed the next day. When I came straight home from work (I wasn't even stopping at Dixie's after my shift anymore), the house was empty. Betty and Joe were gone. And all Betty's clothes and toiletries and romance novels were gone, too.

After rushing around the house like a madman, I found a note pinned to the pillow on my side of the bed, in Betty's neat handwriting:

Dear Donald,

As you should have figured out by now, I left with Joe Reed. It's really for the best. You have to believe that. Maybe it was always meant to be that I would end up with him, even after he died. It was as if my soul was as dead as his when you brought him home. Now, maybe, we can resurrect our lives and start all over again. Even you. I don't think you really ever loved me. That's why you drank so much. Maybe now you will stop drinking and find someone who can make you happy like I never could.

So don't be sad. This change will be good for both of us, for all of us. I feel confident, I really do, that we are going to find our souls.

Love,
Betty

I read the note a couple more times then let it drop to the bed. What a weird way life has in getting us what we always wanted. I now know Betty had always wanted Joe and I had been the consolation prize.

Incessant banging shook me out of my head. Someone was at my front door. A moment later, they crashed through. When I ran out to the living room, I was tackled by a couple skinny army privates.

"Hold him down!" urged a red-faced, granite-headed sergeant.

Within moments, a few other privates were reporting that the rest of the house was secure. The sergeant scowled and gestured to the sofa.

"Sit him there!" he barked.

The privates dragged me over to the sofa, and held me down.

The sergeant leaned his granite face into mine. "Where is he?"

"Who?"

"The zombie!"

I shrugged and almost laughed. It was funny to have to tell him that the "zombie" had run off with my wife.

Dr. Hurlburt came to see me after a few days. I had been whisked off to some secret army base and questioned for hours at a time by several mean-spirited agents who seemed to doubt every essence of my being. Some of them got impatient and shouted I was a traitor. Others used the kind approach, trying to be my buddy. Others used threats.

Homeless Zombies

I told them all the same thing: the truth. I didn't know where that zombie, Joe Reed, was. He had run off with my wife.

"They are never gonna believe that story," said Dr. Hurlburt. He was beaming with a kind smile, as if he were innocent in all of this.

"But it's true," I told him.

"They can't believe a zombie could ever fall in love," he said.

That hurt. Joe Reed and Betty in love.

"But, it's true, I tell you," I said. "It's true."

Dr. Hurlburt sighed. "So," he said, "they do have souls."

I nodded. I had found out the hard way.

"But they're still homeless," I told him. "I guess."

Dr. Hurlburt looked at me and smiled. "Aren't we all," he told me with a wink.

THE VALACE STANDARD

by

RYAN C. THOMAS

NOW

The windows in my living room overlook the courtyard, a large square of green grass synthed from silk and monofilament so soft it's like walking on cotton balls. In the center, four marble fish leaping from a marble wave spit water into a small reflecting pool. Surrounding this are paved footpaths and wrought iron benches, rhododendrons and hydrangea. A koi pond resides near the community garden, which sits against the South Tower. It truly is a serene courtyard, a postcard-perfect recreation of a pristine suburban American park.

I used to sit out there in the courtyard and write my notes. It's where I came up with the code for my greatest software creation. The ersatz sunlight generated on the vapor screen high above head, coupled with the heat rods hidden in the upper ledges, means it is summer all year round. Perfect for thinking. Perfect for creating.

Right now, a family of three is running across the courtyard to the door of the West Tower. I see it's Craig Richardson, his wife and daughter from 55D. Richardson has a rifle; he cocks it. A Reclamation, something ungodly fast and once human, races after them. Richardson turns and fires, sending a bullet through the creature's head. It drops and its velocity causes it to slide headfirst into the fountain, a mixture of blood and brain spitting up the base. It continues to twitch.

I squeeze my fists tight and say a prayer for them; I like the Richardsons, I know them well. They hit the door and key in their passcode, but it doesn't open. They start pounding on it, waving frantically at the omniEye set in the wall next to it. Still nothing happens. Mandy, the daughter, my son's former girlfriend—a sweet girl blossoming into an incredibly beautiful woman—is crying hysterically. She is covered in blood and I realize that the fourth member of their

138

family, her baby brother David, is not with them. Faintly, I can hear Danielle, Richardson's wife, screaming about a key. But there is no backup key for the West Tower door. There are no backup keys for any of the doors. Everyone signed that away when they accepted living here. No methods for the homeless, penniless dregs to get in. Our Manhattan Castle—safe, secure, walled off from the rest of the city.

Danielle kicks the door; Mandy cries hysterically as she looks over her shoulder toward the fountain; Richardson aims his rifle at the door but doesn't pull the trigger. He knows it will be a waste of ammo; all the doors are blast proof. Can I maneuver my way through the corridors and get down there to let them in before—

No. Four Reclamations explode out from nearby windows, two stories up, shards of glass firing out everywhere. The creatures land hard and are instantly running full speed, their milk-white eyes focused with the rage of Lyssa. They are hunters, their muscles newly repaired and improved, their insides taut and youthful despite their outward decay. I have yet to see anyone outrun them. I know what is coming, but still I watch and hope a miracle will happen.

Richardson screams, terrified. He fires the gun. The bullet misses the Reclamation leaping for him and punches through his teenage daughter's face. It explodes the hinge of her jaw and her mouth falls open like a broken suitcase, spilling her tongue out across her neck. She falls to the ground, her hands grasping air. One of the undead is on her instantly, ripping through her flesh. Danielle freezes, is tackled by two creatures at once, hit so hard her legs fly parallel to the ground as she rams into the door. A howling fury of undead fingernails, teeth, and gouging fingers tear at her. The creatures swarm like nanobots on a cancer, engulf this family, shred them to ribbons. Scraps of flesh sail through the air. The gun goes off again, strikes the bricks near my window and I flinch. Before I can recover I see Richardson's head flung up against the North Tower wall. It connects with a forceful splat and the eyes burst from their sockets. Mandy's lower leg is arced into the fountain, a kite tail of meaty gristle trailing behind it. Her intestines are whipped into the koi pond. Danielle simply erupts in a mist of blood, as if C4 had been packed in her spine. These warrior undead shred her with jet-engine speed. It—

It's over in four seconds and the Reclamations are scaling the walls back up to the tempered windows of the third floor. They smash their decaying heads against the glass in complete synchronized form, shatter the windows, and race back inside the building. The courtyard is silent again. There is nothing left of the bodies, just a mess of pink and red against the walls. I thank God one of them did not choose my window.

I close the blinds, pour myself a highball and sit back down in my recliner. I can hear them bellowing throughout the building, these monsters, like bad blood in dying veins, tearing it apart in a frantic search for me and anything else living. Their echoes come through the vents, accompanied by screams of pain and death. Time is short.

Instead of running, I pick up the handheld bot scanner from the end table and move its sensor over my forearm, watch as the screen magnifies the medical nanobug attached to my ulna. Like a spider wrapping up a moth, its microscopic legs beat themselves against my bone. Repairing something? Quickly, I pick up the jackknife, also laying on the end table, and flick the blade open. I take a big swig of whiskey and then pour the rest of it over my forearm. Without thinking I jam the blade through my flesh, careful to avoid the artery, and slice a chunk of meat away. I'm wailing. The bone is exposed, a pearly scale in an eddy of liberated blood. I scrape the blade against it, flecking bone dust into my lap. The pain is unbelievable, and instantly I feel faint.

I wave the scanner over the flayed flesh and bone chips on my bloody lap. Its sangria display screen reveals the bug moving in circles. I drop the whiskey glass and head to the bathroom to flush the flesh and bug down the toilet. I wrap my arm in gauze from the bathroom first aid kit. A stab from a morphine hypo numbs me and now it's not just pain that makes me feel woozy.

I must stay awake, however. I need to get to the penthouse. The Castle, and the future of mankind, depends on it. I pick up the scanner again and head for the door.

THEN

The Castle was built in 2012, at the northern tip of Manhattan. It's just a castle in name, obviously. In truth it is a fully-loaded apartment complex, complete with state of the art security and self-sustaining amenities such as a grocery store, bank, gym, spa, restaurant, coffee house, computer café, etc. It houses only two hundred units, each of which requires a certain stature in life for renting.

Marshall Valace owned the entire top floor penthouse, since he was, after all, the man who built the building. Valace's family fortune was made in real estate. It was his father who developed the Urban Castle design, which soon graced fourteen major centers around the globe, including London, Dubai, Moscow, Los Angeles, Chicago, Bangkok, Berlin, and Washington D.C., to name a few. Marshall Valace was richer than the world's banks combined. In fact, he'd inherited many of them when is father, Calvin Valace, died.

Unlike his father, Marshall's focus was technology. But the apple never falls too far from the tree—some of that technology was geared toward real estate, just not on Earth. "We've developed what we can here. Our future is out there. We just need the elbow grease to get it done. If we can dream it, we can build it. That's why you're here. To realize my future. Our future."

These were the words he said to me when I first met him. A sculpted man with a collection of gold rings, he was much smarter than he looked, and he looked handsome enough already. I can't deny I was intimidated, but I stood my ground when it came to my compensation.

"I want full benefits."

"Please. You'll have more than benefits. You'll have everything you've ever wanted. Just tell me you can write the programs I need." He was seated behind his massive cherry wood desk, composed like the definition of success. "I want complete communication between them. The faster and more independent the programs the faster I can get these projects off the ground."

"If your satellites can link them all up," I replied.

"You're questioning my satellites? Son, I own nine-tenths of the satellites up there." He pointed up to the ceiling but I knew what his finger was addressing. "Don't tell me you're doubting me."

"No. Not at all. Just making sure."

"Well get sure. Now, the nanotech program . . . the code can be implemented? This is big money and I've got buyers waiting to throw cash at me."

"Mr. Valace, I come with fifteen years as head of GeneTech's robotics software program—"

"Yes yes! I know you're history. That's why you're here. Stop pretending this is a formal interview. I don't have time for niceties. Can you create the communication programs I need on a micro level as well? I already know your robotics program was a coup for science but it still was segregated. A man told your bots what to do and they did it. I don't want men involved. That divide slows things down. I want the things to just know what to do. Nanotechnology is the future of medicine. I'm talking about intelligent, communicative medicine."

"The size of the machine is not the issue when it comes to the code, Mr. Valace. Once written, the algorithms will allow any computer or processor to retain information and learn from it."

"So my robotics, my programs, will be able to communicate with themselves? I'm talking in every factory. I've got factories all over the world. I need it all linked. Nanotech. Computers. Factory automation. I need it all to work faster. Better. Will your program do that?"

"Sure, like business partners working in tandem."

"But I want them *all* to speak when necessary. If I can get all these machines to manage themselves, work autonomously, well . . . I can really get things done in time. You know about my space program?"

"Yes. I've read about it. You want to send people to Mars?"

"I'll be the first private entrepreneur to get us to another planet come hell or high water but I need the machines to build my product at optimum speed. They need to work faster and better than men, know how to solve problems—"

I nodded. "Trust me, Mr. Valace, if you give me the budget I need, I'll get your program for you. Any programs you need. Your software will be optimized like nothing you've ever seen."

"Because you realize that humans are too slow to get this work done by themselves. I don't want humans involved any more; they screw up too much. A machine does what it's told twenty-four-seven. And I've got too many projects to complete and barely enough time to do them in to rely on overworked men. Valace Technologies is the number one producer of tomorrow's technology. I want it kept that way. Get what I'm saying?"

"Yes, sir."

"Good." He pointed across his cavernous office to the door I'd come through. "Who's that kid there, looking through the glass?"

"My son," I replied. Gavin was on the other side of the door, pressed up against the frosted pane, his hands cupped around his eyes. "I'm sorry, but he's out of school today and when your secretary called this morning to ask me to come in I didn't have enough time to find a sitter. Gavin," I called, "go sit back down. I'll be out in a minute."

"Nonsense," Valace said. "Bring him in. I want to meet him."

Somewhat hesitantly I rose, made my way across the room and let Gavin in. He walked briskly, shouldering the backpack I'd just bought him for school. It was so big it almost dragged him down but he'd insisted he wanted a "big boy" backpack.

Valace waited for us to return and pulled a chocolate drop from his desk. "Here, son. Try this."

Gavin took it with a smile.

"How old are you, boy?"

My son looked to me and when I nodded he responded: "Five years old. No, wait, five and a half. I'll be six in four months."

"My my my, a futurist like myself. Always looking ahead. Your daddy tells me you're in school."

Gavin nodded enthusiastically. "I go to kindergarten. 'Cept today it was closed."

"Closed for parent teacher conferences," I added. I obviously wasn't going to make the meeting.

"Tell me, Gavin, do you like this building?" Valace waved his hand around the room.

Gavin smiled. "It's gigantic. It has vapor screens in the bathrooms!"

"Yes, it does. You never know when news is going to happen. A good businessman is always connected. Would you like to live here someday, Gavin?"

"Yes!"

"Well, you just might, if your daddy can make me happy."

My son looked at me wide-eyed. "Can you, Daddy?"

I didn't like the way Valace was trying to manipulate me through my son. I'd already told him I'd do the work if he was serious about paying me what I wanted. There was no need to goad me. Suddenly I had a bad taste in my mouth. But the truth was I wanted Gavin to have a good life, and Valace could provide that, so I let it go. "Yes, son, I'm going to work with Mr. Valace now. We're going to send people to other planets."

"Cooool."

Valace gave Gavin another chocolate drop and told him to go sit back in the outer office. "Cute kid," he said when we were alone again. "I don't have any myself, but I look at all mankind as my children. You start tomorrow."

And so I wrote the program, and Valace's machines were linked together across the ether, sending messages through wireless satellite connections, working twenty-four hours non-stop without the need of much human interaction. They talked to each other, they could remember and learn from their mistakes. If machine A broke, machine B came to its aid, and machine C filled in.

Valace Industries doubled its production of electronics in the first year. By cutting jobs formerly filled by humans and replacing them with the newly "intelligent" robotics, running on my software, the company was also able to double profits, which it then poured back into its R and D department. By the time Gavin was eight, my program was running every aspect of Valace Industries. To us, looking at it from a profit angle, it was pure success. It became known as the Valace Standard. Everything produced by Valace could communicate amongst itself, run on its own. All we did was collect the money from sales of Valace Industries products.

Now, don't think I'm stupid. Failsafes were ensured. A program that smart could cause problems. Not AI problems—true AI would be a celebrated event—but problems with the program overriding human commands that it thought were errors.

"I want a code key established," Valace told me. "A way for me to get in and take control if I need to."

"I'll write you a way into the program," I assured him. "Keep it safe. If anyone finds it they could get in and take over the software. This is not open source stuff."

"Anyone touches my software I will end them. Just write it."

And I did—the failsafe. A code for Valace. A separate code for myself.

Meanwhile, production increased tenfold. Twentyfold. Thirtyfold. Valace had the market on technology, from the smallest comphone to the largest robotic dock arm. All assembled and supported free of human interaction, thanks to the Standard.

When Gavin was ten, I had made Mr. Valace enough money to buy entire continents. We finally moved into the Manhattan Castle and Valace announced he was ready to send the first manned rocket to Mars.

I opted for the quaint three-bedroom in the North Tower with its courtyard view because I liked peace and quiet; I knew I'd get no work done looking out over the city. What was there to look at, anyway? The crumbling facades of abandoned apartment buildings, now mere skeletons with broken walls and shattered windows open to the environments. I couldn't stand looking into those empty apartments. Like looking into the wounds of corpses. All those wires and struts, pipes and rebar, pointing accusatorily back at me. But the buildings weren't the worst. No. It was the homeless. They were everywhere, begging, yelling, crying. A man couldn't work with such a view.

But I'm getting ahead of myself.

Five years had passed since I'd unleashed my software creation. Five years of massive automated productivity, of people losing their jobs while robots and computers took over. Five years of a failing job market generated by my success.

Valace had enough influence now that he practically owned D.C. The president was a regular guest at the Manhattan Castle and, I later found out, had his own unit reserved for whenever he felt like dropping in.

He was there for the first meeting concerning the Exit Pods. I got called down from my new home to talk shop with him and Marshall.

"George, get over here, I want you to meet President Santiago."

The old man looked just as he did in the daily news feeds. White hair with black specks over the ears. A healthily tanned face. Thin, tall, in his customary gray suit. His bank account was one tenth what Valace's was, which always made me question his intentions with my boss.

I extended my hand, slightly awed, and he shook it. Standing at varying intervals throughout the room were five men in dark gray suits. Their eyes were solid black—scanner lenses. I recognized them because Valace Industries made them. Craig Richardson came up with the design and I wrote the software for them. They were see-through, but with a simple whispered voice command would register heat signatures, x-ray a room, record and playback a full five minutes of video (or video files on the net), call up data from a number of government server banks. They were creepy as anything but Santiago's people paid us a nice little sum for them.

Valace looked at me. "George, the president and I have a problem and we need your help. But first I need you to understand that what we discuss in this room is just between the three of us."

"Sure." I nodded. "You know me by now, Marshall."

"I do. And that's why you're here. You take your paycheck and don't ask questions. I give you a good life here. I expect that to continue."

"It will. Gavin and I are enjoying our new life here. It's . . . perfect."

"But out there it's anything but perfect." Santiago pointed out the large window behind Valace's desk. The city, shrouded in the smog and decay of our factories' continual production schedule, looked back at us. "Crime is up. People are struggling. Homelessness has never been more prevalent. You guys put a lot of people out of work. The divide is great."

"A casualty of economics," Valace offered. "Or perhaps just a necessary, long overdue change. What say you, George?"

I looked away from the window. "I'm not sure I follow."

Valace lit a cigar, moved to the window and stared out. "We have made incredible strides. We are about to go to Mars. As soon as the nanobots are perfected, lifespans will increase dramatically and we'll be able to populate that distant world without fear of disease. Even here, the necessary people will endure, contribute to society for twice as long. A hundred years ago people died in their sixties and seventies, now they will easily live to one hundred and ten, one hundred and fifteen."

"Those that can afford it." The president punctuated his statement with a raised index finger.

"Precisely my point. We do not work for free. That's the way the world works. The strong survive, flourish, reproduce. Yet, we're made to feel selfish for this." He pointed out the window to the ruins and homeless mobs outside the Castle walls. "Why? The lower class siphons while the rest of us work to make the world a better place. Why should we be expected to pull them out of their bogs? Why must it be our responsibility?"

I gestured toward the president. "Well, I guess it's his."

Valace turned around and met my eyes. "George, the president and I here have been discussing an alternative to the despondency . . . overtaking the nation's unemployed and homeless."

"Oh, hush, Marshall. You're treating the man like a child. Talk straight."

Valace cleared his throat. "George, the president can't take care of all the sick and hungry. Nor am I obligated to. Times have changed. We'll soon be on Mars but we still have business here a while longer. Effective reform for the homeless would bankrupt the nation and everything we've worked for. They need to go."

"Wait." My jaw dropped. "Are you suggesting—"

"We're not suggestion anything."

"Let me handle this," the president said. "George, we help the ones we can. But our deficit is high. Our debts are astronomical."

"Borrow money."

"Oh we've borrowed enough money. No, the people want a way out. They know full well we can't give them a better life. We can barely give them food and shelter. And what food and shelter we do give them isn't very tasteful. Do you know what the current suicide rate is?"

I turned to my benefactor. "But, Marshall, you could help. You could fund a project to—"

"I'm not funding any project but the ones I want to. And right now I am putting all my chips on Mars. With your software and my capital we'll establish the first American city on another planet. Think about that."

President Santiago stepped closer. "We're on board with Marshall here. We want Mars. And despite Valace Technologies' private status, we see it as a win for all of America. These dregs that line the streets out there . . . . Look, times are different. We can't help them beyond what we can afford to dole out to them bit by bit."

I shook my head. "So what are we talking about? You said they want a way out . . . ?"

"They do. And we're gonna give it to them. Tomorrow I'm drafting a bill for Congress. Legal suicide."

"You're kidding. It'll never pass."

"Sure it will. Marshall owns half the yammering lobbyists on the hill and I'm sure he'll grease some palms as well. It's going to go through. Maybe not right away but soon enough. Relax, you look upset. We're not talking about killing people. We're giving them an option. They'll have to sign all the forms, testify on video, have legal witnesses, yadda yadda yadda. George, they *want* this. They're jumping off buildings and overdosing on drugs by the minute. There's no work for most of them. I have no jobs to give them. This way we can ease their pain."

"Nobody *wants* this," I insisted.

Marshall put his hand on my shoulder. "Nevertheless, they're going to keep offing themselves. So we'll charge a small fee, give them a painless way out, and we'll kick back some profit to the boys in the Whitehouse. George, I want you to invent the machine. Keep it in line with our style, you know, automated. Take care of the software. The usual routine. I'll pay you *triple* your salary. Can you do it?"

"Me? What about Richardson—"

"I've got him busy on other stuff. Just answer me."

A long silence overtook me, during which I thought long and hard about my answer. My software had made me financially comfortable, but had already put so many out of work. Now I would be the man to put them in the grave. But I would be a liar to say my thoughts didn't drift toward further financial gain. Gavin would be set for life, and I could retire early. If what they were saying was true, if people wanted it and would willingly sign the requisite forms, then why should I feel like I was in the wrong? The world was overcrowded, and so many contributed nothing to society. People were free to make their own choices, right? Maybe it was time to give them a better option than pills and bullets.

"Okay, Marshall. I'll come up with something."

"Good man. I knew you'd come through."

The bill was passed. The Exit Pods worked effectively and painlessly. People lined up by the thousands. The Vatican attacked us in the papers and millions protested, but what did we care? I went from comfortable to wealthy, planned on retiring as soon as Gavin graduated. Then, three years later . . . the Reclamation Pits. What a mess. Valace tried to squash it but the news teams were persistent. Fact was, it was news to me as well. Why had Valace kept it from me? It took Gavin to later explain it all to me. Leave it to our youth to find alternate ways of getting the truth. But again, I'm ahead of myself. Gavin's distrust came first.

"I saw you in the news today, Dad," he said, coming back from the third-floor high school one day. "Mandy Richardson showed it to me. It said you ruined the stock market. It said something about you being the father of suicide."

I turned off the news feed and shut down the vapor screen. The images of all the dead still swam through my mind. "We're successful, Gav. Some people just don't like it when other people get ahead."

He threw his book bag on the couch and grabbed a juice from the fridge. "Not true," he said, coming back into the living room. "Mandy's dad was in the news, too. They said his invention is 'the new fountain of youth.' They mean the nano thingies, I think. So nobody is mad at him."

"Craig's nanobots are revolutionizing medicine, Gav. But they run on my program. They'll attack cancerous cells and repair damaged tissue, whatever they find, but they can only do it by communicating with one another. I made that happen. The Valace Standard, remember?"

"The news reels didn't mention that. Just said Mr. Richardson's invention is, like, some crazy special advancement of science."

"Well, that because the nanobots *are* special. They're the first ones that can reproduce at their own will. It's a big deal for Mr. Richardson and for Valace Technologies."

"Why do they reproduce?"

"Any number of reasons. Maybe one is damaged and wants to replace itself. Maybe one needs help attacking a rapidly replicating virus and has to call in some help. The nanobots can heal people faster if there are more of them."

"And your program lets them do that?"

"Well, Mr. Richardson came up with the mechanism that allows them to copy themselves into new bots . . . but they still communicate through my software. And the best part is they can do it on their own. They don't have to wait for someone to tell them to fix what they find. They just do it, talk amongst themselves. That's my program." I smiled triumphantly.

"Yeah, and now doctors are out of work, most people can't even afford the nano things, homeless are offing themselves because there are no jobs, and you're some kind of benevolent god, right?" Gavin stormed off to his room.

"Gavin! We're preparing to move civilization to other planets. It'll make life better for everyone."

But the truth was plain as day outside the Castle, in the crumbling city. Exit Queues were through the roof, and our special brand of medical care was not cheap. Each nanobot implantation cost upwards of eighty thousand dollars. Of course it was worth it. A single nanobot could stay in your system for over fifty years, constantly fighting off problems, creating more nanobots if the need arose. People were going to live longer. At least, the ones that could afford it.

Both myself and Gavin had been injected with a nanobot at our last physical, though I was ordered by Marshall to keep it secret. Gavin didn't even know he had one in him. Richardson's kids didn't either. But nobody had been ill since.

I looked at Gavin's room and thanked God he would never have to want for anything. It was for his future I had written my program. It was for him I blocked the news file every morning.

In July of Gavin's senior year of high school, we launched the first Valace Shuttle to Mars. It crashed on the surface near the Valles Marineris and all the crew died. It was a major failure for Valace Industries and sent Marshall into a severe depression. The press made him a pariah, plastered his face all over the net along with the faces of the dead—ten married couples. His spin doctors might have turned it around but the press had just revealed the news about the Reclamation Pits, and this only set him over the edge. I didn't see him for many months afterward.

I had expected to be fired, or at least blamed for the disaster, but it turned out to be human error—wrong landing coordinates.

But for me, that wasn't the worse problem: Gavin had disappeared. Ever since the Reclamation Pits had been discovered he wouldn't talk to me. Our last conversation burned in my head:

"You used people! You manipulated them and killed them and used them!"

"I did no such thing. Mr. Valace gave people an option. A very legal option."

"He gave people an option? No, he didn't. He made them believe it was the only way out. And you gave him the means to cash in on it. You told me the bodies were cremated."

"No, I didn't. People have the option of burial, too."

"Bull, Dad." Gavin rarely talked back to me, and normally I'd have scolded him but he was a grown man now and had every right to be angry. I'd been just as angry when I found out what Marshall had been doing with the bodies.

"I didn't know about the Pits, Gav. Honest."

"Would it have mattered? You'd have still built the Exit Pods." He paused, walked into his room and came out a minute later carrying a backpack, the one he'd been wearing to school all these years. The one I bought him for kindergarten. "I'm leaving, Dad. I can't stay here. You're blind to what you have become. But out there, outside, there are people who need real help, not stupid gadgets and rockets. I won't let you ruin my life anymore."

"What are you talking about? You're one of the wealthiest teenagers on the planet right now. I did this all for you. Gav, the people out there have made their choices. I worked hard to give us all of this. It's for you."

"I don't want it. People hate us."

I punched the wall. "What have they been teaching you in that school!"

"Nothing but lies, if you must know. Nothing but history rewritten by your boss. But I got a real education. Me, Mandy, all of us. You can't hide the truth anymore. We find our news like the rest of the world. We seek it out from the places you can't silence. From the people you put out of work, the people you've killed. We know the truth about the Reclamation Pits. We know how you stacked the bodies in the Pits and let them rot. How you collected the gasses as they decomposed and used it to fuel your factories. Your machines and computers and industry ate up the Earth's fuel so you found a new source: people. You put them out of work, made them suffer, made them believe they were better off dead. All so you could harness some methane and hydrogen and use it to get to Mars. But it didn't work!"

"That was all Marshall! I didn't know!"

"So you've said. Either way . . . your machines killed them. Your other machines used them. The only machines this company created to save people nobody can afford. Nobody except the people Valace wants to go to Mars. His new race of space traveling billionaires. It's disgusting. The people outside this building—sorry, *compound*—hate us. And we're not on Mars. We're here, with an angry populace waiting to kill us."

I couldn't deny that. The press, the people, had turned against Valace Industries. They called the Reclamation Pits an atrocity. I swear I didn't know. Worse, Valace still hadn't shut them down, said he was waiting for a court ruling. The rest of the world compared us to the Nazis. But I was only trying to do good, to provide for my family and help further the future of our race.

Gavin opened the door and left. I let him go. I figured he'd spend the night with a friend and come back cool in the morning. But he didn't come back.

A month later I got a letter in the mail. It was addressed from the Valace Industries Exit Program and was accompanied by a small plastic box. I knew what it was; I'd developed the program that mailed them. The letter informed me that Gavin had taken his own life in one of our Exit Pods. The form said the accompanying box contained his belongings. It also said it contained his ashes, but what it really contained, if the press was right, was burned roadkill. Gavin was likely rotting in one of the Pits somewhere.

I fell to my knees and wailed. Later, I discovered in his belongings, a scrap of paper with my Standard override code written on it.

NOW

I open the door to the hallway and peek outside. The lights are off and there is blood smeared along the walls. A severed leg rests like rolled up dough against the baseboard. At the end of the hall a shadow darts out of one of the apartments and bolts through the double doors opposite it. I hear it jumping down the stairwell. I know it is a Reclamation when I hear it howl on the way down. It is a miracle it doesn't see or smell me.

The morphine sets my insides itching and I stumble as I walk, but I hold myself up against the wall and make my way toward the elevator. The bot scanner scrapes against the wall as I move. Time is short and I need to get to Valace's penthouse office; it is the only unit above the labs with direct access to the satellites. According to my systems check, the labs are destroyed, awash in blood.

I come to a T-intersection and go right. The backup lighting starts to flicker and buzz. Halfway down I stop and throw up. The Reclamations have caught people here and finished them off. I count six heads. It looks like someone blew them up with dynamite. I put my hand over my mouth and slosh through the bloody goo.

The elevators have a backup power source that runs on stored solar energy; Valace was petrified that he might have to get down in an emergency and wasn't about to walk down ten flights of stairs. Only a handful of people know the code to run the lifts this way. I'm one of them.

I punch the code into the keypad. The elevator doors open and I step inside, key the code to ascend.

"Wait! Hold the doors!"

Through the closing doors I see a man and woman running my way through the carnage. I thrust my hand forward to hold the doors for them but stop when I see two Reclamations burst after them from around the corner. The creatures sprint with lightning speed, leap through the air with nails flared and teeth bared. They land on the two terrified Valace Industry workers and eviscerate them, like someone shooting bullets through plums. Entrails suddenly drip from the ceiling. The creatures look up. See me. Bolt for the closing elevator doors. Their dead bodies and rotten flesh slam into the other side, bulging the metal inward like a giant welt. Their shrieks cut through the walls.

Then I'm rising, and praying.

The doors open into Marshall's office. The lights wink on and off, the furniture has been overturned. A vapor screen is on to a local news channel. The live footage comes from a helicopter hovering over the city, filming the streets below as people run willy-nilly trying to get away from the raging undead.

For a second I stop and watch, mesmerized by the carnage and destruction. Then one of them walks through the vapor screen's mist, sees me and lunges.

I jump to my left, slide over Marshall's desk and hit the red button underneath. Instantly, red beams separate the desk from the rest of the room, a security device Marshall had installed ages ago. The Reclamation hits the beams and bounces back, a lattice work of fresh electrical burns cooking its flesh.

The creature looks . . . confused. It tries again and is met with the same result. If it tries to run all the way through the beams they will slice it to pieces. Does it know this? It must because it doesn't try again, just howls and leers at me.

Its flesh is gray and eroded, the face stained with ichor, but I see its muscles rippling beneath the tattered clothes. He is undead, but something more, something else. A Reclamation, his body even now being repaired and upgraded.

Tentatively, I step forward to the beams, a foot away from the monster on the other side, and wave the scanner at it. As I suspect, millions of nanobots scurry about its system, fixing the dead tissue, repairing everything. They have reproduced at an alarming rate. They communicate so efficiently, fixing things faster than any human doctor ever could . . . if a human doctor could figure out how to bring the dead back to life.

And now my suspicions fall into place. These undead are a product of all my work, of Gavin's depression and hate. The nanobots have gotten into the Reclamation Pits when Gavin killed himself. Then they started repairing the decaying corpses. But why do they want to kill?

Now I see the leftovers of a body to my right, an arm and an ear. I see Marshall's remains spattered in the corner. Like the others, he's been torn to bits.

I move back to the desk, key in my personal password, and call up the visual on the vapor screen. The news switches to the computer's desktop view and the data for the satellite link . . . and reveals my worst fear. I am denied access to the system. I've come here to key in my override code and manually input the shutdown command for anything using the Valace Standard. But of course it doesn't work. Richardson already told me what Gav told Mandy when he split. He wanted to get back at me, destroy the Valace Standard so automated production would fail and people would be able to work again. But this is the opposite! He never shut it down; instead he opened a universal link. Is that why he killed himself? He failed? He has opened the floodgates of communication, allowed the nanobots a link to—

"We are coming for you."

I step back, frozen. It can speak! The creature's inhuman voice carries with it a threat on a cosmic level.

"Who are you? What do you want?"

"Want your world. Kill you first. Then come. Then our world."

On the vapor screen there's the path of the signal, carrying messages to the nanobots in the undead bodies. A universal signal being carried to every nanobot, every machine using the Valace Standard. It does not originate from any of the computers here on Earth.

It's being relayed through the crashed shuttle on Mars!

"Who are you?" I know that whatever controls the nanobots inside this thing, whatever looks back at me, is not human. It's alien. Communicating to us through space, through the shuttle's link. Something on Mars. Something we missed all these years while thinking the planet was uninhabited. Something we never saw, or can't see, or didn't think to look for. Something intelligent and evil.

I need to shut down the nanobots but the Valace Standard has been hijacked. I try to access the nanobot command console through the scanner but again am denied access. I try a dozen other ways to get admin access to any program to take control of the software. I am denied at every turn. Finally, the comdesk shuts down. The vapor screen goes blank. The Reclamation stares back at me, biding its time. How long before all the power goes out?

From here, I can still see out the giant window overlooking the city. Below me, the dead run about with terrible speed, streaks of gray followed by tiny bursts of red. One of the blood-covered creatures looks like Gavin, but I can't be sure.

Another creature rushes into the office. Probably called by the one that was already here. So I laugh. An alien invasion by way of dead humans. And they didn't even have to come to our planet to do it. They just used . . . me.

My advancements. My greed. My dead.

THOSE UNDEAD WRITERS

Gustavo Bondoni is a winner of the National Space Society's "Return to Luna" contest, as well as a 2008 Marooned Award for flash fiction and has had over forty short stories published in five countries and two languages. His first reprint collection, *Tenth Orbit and Other Stories*, is due in late 2009 from Cyberwizard Productions, and a short novel is due from Daverana Enterprises. You can read his thoughts at http://bondo-ba.livejournal.com

Eric S. Brown is the author of the upcoming releases: *World War of the Dead, Season of Rot* and *Barren Earth*. Some of his past works include *Cobble, Madmen's Dreams,* and *Unabridged Unabashed and Undead: The Best of Eric S. Brown* among others. His short fiction has been published hundreds of times and he was featured as an expert on the walking dead in the book, *Zombie CSU*. Eric is thirty-four years old and lives in N.C. with his loving wife, Shanna, and his son, Merrick.

Michael Cieslak is a life-long reader and writer of all forms of speculative fiction. He is a member (and former officer) of the Great Lakes Association of Horror Writers. He can be found at thedragonsroost.net and various social networking sites, especially his current addiction—Twitter.

Lorne Dixon lives and writes somewhere off an exit of Route 78 in residential New Jersey. He grew up on a diet of yellow-spined paperbacks, black and white monster movies, and the thunder lizard backbeat of rock 'n' roll. His novella, *Snarl*, is now available from Coscom Entertainment.

A.P. Fuchs lives in Winnipeg, Manitoba, where he writes superhero and zombie fiction. His superhero character, Axiom-man, can be found at www.apfuchs.com, while his undead work can be found at www.undeadworldtrilogy.com

Anthony Giangregorio is the author of more than twenty novels, almost all of them about zombies. He has a story in the upcoming zombie anthology by Library of the Living Dead Press and another one *in Dead Worlds: Undead Stories* by Living Dead Press. Check out his website at www.undeadpress.com

Glen Held lives on Long Island with his wonderful wife and three great kids, none of whom are, or intend to be, zombies. Glen has a mystery/romance novel, *Burning Secrets,* to his credit and is currently writing an urban fantasy.

Becca Morgan is a third generation geek, the daughter of a game designer and a horror writer. She's grown up preparing for the zombie apocalypse and will probably be voted "Most Likely to Raise the Dead" when she gets to high school.

Mark Onspaugh is a native Californian who grew up on a steady diet of horror, science fiction and DC Comics. A proud member of the HWA, he writes screenplays, short stories and novels. He lives in Los Osos, C.A. with his wife, author/artist Dr. Tobey Crockett. See www.markonspaugh.com for more.

Gina Ranalli is the author of several books, including *Sky Tongues, Chemical Gardens, Mother Puncher* and *Wall of Kiss,* among others. You can visit her on the web at www.ginaranalli.com

Vincent L. Scarsella has gained success in publishing his work in such magazines as *The Leading Edge, Aethlon: The Journal of Sport Literature, Fictitious Force* and *Aphelion.* He may be contacted by email at vscarsella@roadrunner.com. He is also set to publish a non-fiction self-help book for humanity, *The Human Manifesto: A General Plan for Human Survival,* based upon the writings of Ernest Becker. The book has its own web site at www.thehumanmanifestosite.com

Jason Shayer joined the ranks of Canada's horror writers in 2008 and looks to bring Canadian myths and monsters back to life through his dark tales. His twelve-year-old mind frame have given more than a few people a reason to raise an eyebrow, most often his wife. When he's not writing or reading, he's teaching his three-year-old daughter the finer points of zombie lore.

Ryan C. Thomas is the author of the novels *The Summer I Died* and *Ratings Game*. His stories have appeared in numerous markets including *Undead: Headshot Quartet, Space Squid, Nanbison, Hallow's Eve, The Vault of Punk Horror* and more. He works as a journalist in San Diego and can be found in the bars on the weekends playing with his band, The Buzzbombs. Visit him online at www.ryancthomas.com

Adam J. Whitlatch is the author of several science fiction and horror short stories, as well as the novels *The Blood Raven: Retribution* and *E.R.A. - Earth Realm Army*. His works of fiction have appeared in *Six Sentences, Northern Haunts: 100 Terrifying New England Tales, Shroud Magazine,* and *Crossed Genres* to name a few. Adam lives in southeast Iowa with his wife, Jessica, and their two sons. See www.adamjwhitlatch.com for more.

Coscom Entertainment
presents

Book One of the *Undead World Trilogy*

BLOOD
OF THE
DEAD

by

A.P. FUCHS

Excerpt

JOE BAILEY
ZOMBIE HUNTER

"Whattsa matter, baby? Never made love to a zombie before?"

The man's voice was filled with sarcasm but, looking on from the shadows, Joe Bailey couldn't help but think the guy meant every word and that he truly did want the girl to mess around with the dead man in front of her.

The girl, a blonde of probably seventeen or eighteen, frantically tugged at the iron collar around her neck. Joe knew that getting it off would be impossible. The collar was attached to a long iron rod. On the other end was the guy who wanted to see her come apart at the prospect of defiling herself with the undead.

Who knew what they had already done to her before now. What was once an off-yellow dress was mere tatters sagging off her frame like a torn shower curtain. Her cries were muffled by the band of silver duct tape across her mouth. From where Joe lurked off to the side, he could see how her long blonde hair had been pulled forward across her cheeks and stuffed into her mouth to help keep her quiet.

The air stank with booze and dope and the funk of the dead.

The man holding the rod jerked it to the right and left, whipping the girl side to side as he steered her toward the dead man across the basement floor. Four of his friends looked on, yipping and cheering. All five men were eager for what was about to happen. Three were on one side of the room, including the man holding the pole; two were across the way, both gripping a similar iron pole. This one was attached to another collar, one clamped around the neck of an overweight gray-skinned man with a blood-stained white shirt, brown dress pants and only one shoe. The fat man, Joe supposed, had probably been a hard worker when he was alive. Though he was now dead but somehow back to life, he still carried a look of innocence in his eyes, a look of pleading behind the rage and mindless hunger that consumed him.

The jerks cackled and cheered and stepped closer as their buddy forced the girl toward the monster, the dead man trying to step forward with arms outstretched, wanting to grab her. The two guys holding the zombie at bay fought with each tug against the pole. It was a wonder the zombie didn't spin around and take those guys out in an effort to break free. Then again, intelligence was never in a zombie's favor. Joe had been around them long enough to know that much.

Joe remained in the shadows behind an old furnace off to the side. The creeps holding the girl hadn't heard him break in through the first floor window of the house and sneak down the stairs into the shadows, each too consumed with the idea of bringing this girl to the edge of torment and despair before, finally, shoving her off the edge.

"Oh come on, girlie-girlie. It ain't so bad," her captor said. "The dude's just hungry, that's all. You know as well as I do that they need to eat now and then, just like anyone else."

The girl's muffled screams, grunts and heavy breathing through her nose sent a shockwave of apprehension through the air.

The guy holding the iron rod shook off his beaten leather jacket, first his right arm then, after switching his hold on the rod to the other hand, his left. He wore a blue T-shirt, one which reminded Joe of what the sky used to look like before it had permanently clouded over in a sickly mix of gray and brown.

"Whoo-hoo-hoo-hoo-hoo!" Blue T-shirt sang. "One, two, the dead's coming for you!"

The girl screeched behind her gag. Blue's friends howled. They shoved each other playfully like drunks.

"Ready, Betty?" Blue asked.

If "Betty" was the girl's real name or not, Joe didn't know nor, right now, care.

He cursed himself for sitting in the shadows so long, having to watch as Betty inched toward her doom, but if he didn't time this just right, neither he nor she would make it out of here alive. You didn't have to be paranoid to know that each of the men were packing heat, something that had become commonplace once the dead had taken over.

The zombie snarled and a gob of bloody-spit spilled from the corner of its mouth. It violently lurched forward, catching the men holding the iron rod off guard. A muffled *pop* came from the zombie's neck. It had broken it from the force of the pull.

And it still kept moving.

The men holding it at bay yanked back on the rod, jerking the dead man back a step. The zombie grunted, but kept its feet firmly planted so it only leaned back against the air at an impossible angle before tugging itself upright again. The dudes holding the rod lost their grip and the second the iron rod clanged against the concrete floor, the girl screamed, muffled and scared.

"You idiots!" Blue shouted. Indecisiveness flashed across his eyes. He wasn't sure what to do.

Joe pulled the large X-09 to shoulder height, cocked the enormous hammer, and got ready. As was his custom, he counted to three then kissed the tip of the thick barrel before settling his finger around the trigger. One cock of the hammer was good for two shots. He had designed the X-09 himself, a large handgun, black and smooth with a Western flare that packed more punch than a double-barreled shotgun. He could have made a fortune off it if the world was the way it used to be.

But those days were gone.

The zombie scrambled toward the girl. She veered to the side and breathed a shrill wheeze when the collar stopped her stride.

Blue yanked her back then threw her and the pole into the zombie. He and his buddies spun around and ran for the long flight of basement stairs.

Joe jumped out from behind the furnace, aimed at the two yahoos scrambling up the steps in front of Blue and sent a bullet into each of their backs. The sounds of the double gunshot froze Blue in his tracks and by the time he turned around to see the source of fire, Joe had already cocked the hammer again and had the barrel aimed between Blue's eyes.

"What the—" Blue started. He was cut off when the girl shrieked and the zombie, who was now on top of her, growled. "Me or her. What's it gonna be, hero man?"

"Both," Joe said and pulled the trigger.

A blood-red hole the size of a quarter sprang to life at the center of Blue's forehead, the back of his head spraying outward in a rain of flesh and bone. Eyes still gazing at Joe, the dude dropped to his knees then toppled face first onto the floor.

Joe turned and dove to the side as the two guys who had earlier held the zombie at bay aimed their pistols at him and fired. He pulled the trigger in mid air, sending a bullet into the zombie's back, the impact forceful enough to send the dead man rolling off the girl and to the side.

A numby *bang* rocked Joe's shoulder when he hit the ground. Fortunately the long, brown rain-ruined suede trench coat he wore was padded top to bottom so the pain wasn't as sharp as it should have been. He cocked the hammer.

The girl rolled onto her side and tried to get up, but the awkwardness of the neck collar and attached pole screwed up her balance and she fell back down, landing on her stomach and face.

The two men with the pistols opened fire.

Joe sent off two shots, tagging each of them in the heart. Their chests exploded almost simultaneously in a burst of blood and they hit the floor.

The zombie rushed on all fours and tackled the girl, slamming its forehead into the back of her skull. She lay there, still.

Joe got to his feet, cocked the hammer, and took three huge strides over to it. He yanked the dead man up by the collar. The creature turned its head toward him, its bloodshot eyes filled with malice. It reached for Joe's arm.

Joe pulled the trigger.

The shot took off the top of the dead man's head, everything from the eyebrows up. The syrupy splash of brain matter and the soft sound of bone hitting the concrete followed right behind.

Now no longer moving, the dead man's body suddenly weighed a ton and Joe needed both hands to dump it off to the side.

He got down on his knees beside the girl and checked her neck for a pulse. It was there, still frantic from the ordeal.

He turned her over and grimaced at the sight of her bloody face, a deep gouge caused by teeth on her left cheekbone.

"Crap," he muttered.

Her tearstained eyes opened slowly then rolled back in their sockets. When they rolled forward again, a soft smile rose on her face.

"Thanks," she whispered.

Joe stood, sighed, and aimed the gun between her eyes. "You're welcome."

Book One of the *Undead World Trilogy*

BLOOD
OF THE
DEAD

A Shoot 'Em Up Zombie Novel by A.P. Fuchs

"*Blood of the Dead* . . . is the stuff of nightmares . . . with some unnerving and frightening action scenes that will have you on the edge of your seat."

- Rick Hautala
author of *The Wildman*

Joe Bailey prowls the Haven's streets, taking them back from the undead, each kill one step closer to reclaiming a life once stolen from him.

As the dead push into the Haven, he and a couple others are forced into the one place where folks fear to tread: the heart of the city, a place overrun with flesh-eating zombies.

Welcome to the end of all things.

**Ask for it at your local bookstore.
Also available from your favorite on-line retailer.**

ISBN-10   1-897217-80-3 / ISBN-13   978-1-897217-80-1

www.undeadworldtrilogy.com

THE WAR
OF THE
WORLDS
PLUS BLOOD, GUTS AND ZOMBIES
H.G. WELLS AND ERIC S. BROWN

The invasion begins . . .

. . . and the dead start to . . .

RISE

Available at your favorite on-line retailer or local bookstore
ISBN 978-1-897217-91-7

The Hottest Zombie Anthology. The Coolest Authors. The Greatest Stories.

They live. They die. They return.

Zombies.

38 authors. 38 gut-wrenching tales.

Flash fiction at its finest, all illustrated by underground favorite Sean Simmans and edited by Keith Gouveia.

Featuring stories by:

Piers Anthony, Adam-Troy Castro, Nick Cato, Nancy Kilpatrick, Michael Laimo, James Newman, Kurt Newton, Gina Ranalli, Steven Savile, Nate Southard, Jeff Strand, Simon Strantzas, Lee Thomas, Steve Vernon, Tim Waggoner . . . and many others.

Ask for it at your local bookstore.

Also available from your favorite on-line retailer.

ISBN-10 1-897217-81-1 / ISBN-13 978-1-897217-81-8

www.coscomentertainment.com

A Terrifying Werewolf Novella by Lorne Dixon

"Lorne Dixon's *Snarl* will easily fulfill your growing adult werewolf fiction needs."

- W.D. Gagliani,
author of *Wolf's Trap*
and *Wolf's Gambit*

Chev Worke thought he had found a path to easy money. He just didn't count on things going wrong and running into a pack of hungry werewolves.

Barely escaping with his life, Chev learns of a secret pact that has been in place for centuries, the only thing that has kept the town of Easter Glen safe from the bloodthirsty beasts.

There's just one problem: the pact has been broken.

In Easter Glen, by the time you hear a *Snarl*, it's too late.

Ask for it at your local bookstore.
Also available from your favorite on-line retailer.

ISBN-10 1-897217-87-0 / ISBN-13 978-1-897217-87-0

www.coscomentertainment.com

A MISSING BOY. A LONE HERO. A WHOLE LOT OF ZOMBIES.

ISBN 10 - 1-897217-83-8
ISBN 13 - 978-1-897217-83-2

Axiom-man is transported to a world not his own. The streets are empty. There is no one to be found.

Those he does find . . . are dead.

And walking.

Ask for the series at your local bookstore.
Also available at your favorite on-line retailer

Read the whole saga:

1-897217-57-9   978-1-897217-71-9   978-1-897217-69-6

www.axiom-man.com

COSCOM ENTERTAINMENT

Where Imagination is Truth

www.coscomentertainment.com

Zombies, Vampires, and Texans!
Oh, my!
The Novels of Rhiannon Frater

As The World Dies:
The First Days

Two very different women flee into the Texas Hill Country on the first day of the zombie rising. Together they struggle to rescue loved ones, find other survivors, and avoid the hungry undead.

As The World Dies:
Fighting to Survive

Katie and Jenni have found new lives with the survivors of their makeshift safe haven, but danger still lurks. Internal conflicts worsen among the survivors, as the fort is threatened not only by the zombie hordes, but marauding bandits.

Pretty When She Dies
A Vampire Novel

In East Texas, a young woman awakens buried under the forest floor. After struggling out of her grave, she not only faces her terrible new existence but her sadistic creator, The Summoner. Abandoning her old life, she travels across Texas hoping to find answers to her new nature and find a way to defeat the most powerful Necromancer of all time.

All novels are available in both paperback and Kindle on Amazon.com.
eBook versions are available at smashwords.com
For more information on the author, check out her blog at:
http://rhiannonfrater.blogspot.com/

www.ingramcontent.com/pod-product-compliance
Lightning Source LLC
Chambersburg PA
CBHW031245210726

48287CB00003B/910